Shapeshifters at Cilgerran

Dedication

To
my sons
Ivan, Lucas and Jacob

dinas

Shapeshifters
at Cilgerran

Liz Whittaker

Published with the support of the Welsh Books Council

Cover artwork: Jacob Whittaker

ISBN: 0 86243 719 9

Dinas is an imprint of Y Lolfa

Printed and published in Wales
by Y Lolfa Cyf., Talybont, Ceredigion SY24 5AP
e-mail ylolfa@ylolfa.com
website www.ylolfa.com
tel. (01970) 832 304
fax 832 782

CONTENTS

Chapter 1

CONFUSION

'SERIOUS UPSET *in Dreamworld,*' Gido said.

His face was changing as Leo peered at it. One minute he was clear and looking like a human, and the next, he seemed more like some sort of animal, disappearing into a background of trees and dark foliage.

'I can hear you,' Leo called, and his own voice sounded odd, as though he was under water, 'but I can't see you very well.'

'*Tiny worm-hole,*' Gido replied. '*Poor reception, I'm afraid. I'm supposed to be in a dream in Africa right now, but I've heard what's going on in your part of the world, and I'm worried, I can tell you.*'

'What? What's going on?' Leo asked.

'*The Stealers have got control of a bunch of innocents, turned them into troublemakers. I knew it would happen… always knew… you can assist…*'

'I can't,' Leo said with certainty. 'I've got loads of revision to do in the holidays, and my mum and Carl are getting married soon, so I'm going to be very…'

'What? Don't let me down, Leo. You and Ginny are the only people who can help.'

'Ginny won't do it,' Leo said, 'and neither will I.'

A shout from his mother, Rhian, disturbed him. 'Who d'you think you're talking to?' she called up the stairs. 'Get out of bed and stop messing about!'

Leo woke completely. How weird, he thought. He could have sworn he was already awake, and had just closed his eyes for a moment before getting up. He dressed quickly. The brief conversation from his half-sleep would not go away. It had the feel of an interrupted telephone call. There was more to be heard but, obviously, he wasn't going to hear it. It made him feel uncomfortable. He had not forgotten Gido, but it was so long since he'd had any contact with him that it was the last thing he'd expected.

It was over a year since he and Ginny had experienced the horror of encountering one of those whom Gido called 'the Stealers'. Their full name was the Dreamstealers, zombies created by the Cauldron of the Undead, recorded in an historic horror story of which Leo wished he had never heard. Their entire purpose was to turn people into undead like themselves.

Moving between dimensions, they had the power to latch on to people's good dreams and rob them of them. People who fell to their power became empty, and turned to avarice and apathy to try to fill the void inside them. One of these Dreamstealers had met his end at the hands of Gido and his friends, who called themselves the Dreamkeepers, and it was Leo and Ginny who had assisted them and made this possible.

Leo never wanted to meet any of them again. He knew there had originally been three of the Stealers, and that two of them remained at large, but it was not, he told himself as he pulled on his school jersey, his responsibility to dispose of them. If there was trouble in Dreamworld, as Gido had put it, then Gido and his friends could deal with it. The thought of what he and Ginny had gone through raised the hairs on his neck in an unsettling way.

He made his way to the bathroom, splashed his face briefly with water, gave his teeth a quick brush, and went downstairs. Gido sat at the kitchen table.

Leo gaped. 'What are you doing here?' he asked, amazed.

'*Shan't stay long,*' Gido said smoothly. '*I want to talk.*'

'Go away,' Leo said in a panic. 'If my mother sees you here, she'll go mad. I can't explain who you are, or tell her anything.'

'*Must tell you,*' Gido continued, as though Leo hadn't spoken. '*We need you. Desperately need you, unfortunately. Only you can help.*'

Leo sat down and again said, 'Go away,' firmly, as though he meant it.

Gido shook his head. '*Manawl's brooch,*' he said. '*All Dreamworld has known about it for centuries, but no one actually knew where it was. The Stealers think they've found it. I'm furious — especially now they've pulled in the parliament and taken over Cilgerran. Means rescuing the castle as well as the brooch.*'

'Talk sense,' Leo said.

He looked at the table between them. The breakfast cereal label seemed to be different from usual. It said *Pocol Funta* on it.

'I've never heard of that before,' he thought. He picked up the box and shook it. Sounds of squeaking and running feet emerged from the top. He put it down hastily. Something very odd was going on.

'*Just wanted you to know,*' Gido said. '*I suppose, now I've made contact, they'll sniff you out, too. Be warned. Sorry, old bean. Didn't mean to cause you trouble. Got to go. I'll be in touch.*'

With that, he disappeared out of the door.

Leo looked at the cereal box again. He really didn't fancy trying what was inside it.

'I think I'll just have toast,' he said; his voice came very slowly and he could hardly put the words together.

'Make your mind up,' Rhian said.

She was standing at his bedroom door, looking at him as he lay in bed.

'Why aren't you up?'

Leo struggled to the surface. In front of him, he saw the time on his digital alarm showed 7.33.

'Oh no,' he cried, 'I must have gone back to sleep. I dreamed I got up.'

His mother laughed. 'Done it myself before now,' she said. 'Come on. I've got to be out by eight, and I'll give you a lift if you want.'

Leo leapt at top speed to the bathroom. It seemed odd to be doing the same things a second time, and he wondered whether, when he got downstairs, he'd find himself facing Gido again, but he didn't. In addition, the breakfast cereal on the table was, reassuringly, his own favourite, familiar brand. He breathed a sigh of relief. He'd been dreaming. It had been an odd dream, admittedly, but a dream just the same.

'Last day of term,' Rhian said as they left the house. 'Lucky you.'

'Carnival tomorrow, too,' Leo said.

'And only three weeks to go until the wedding,' Rhian said.

Leo's father had died when Leo was six, and he and his mother had lived alone together until she had met Carl, two years ago. Leo liked Carl. He was a pleasant, easy-going man, and Leo was pleased that his mother was marrying him. It made Leo feel less responsible for her. Carl encouraged him in the things he was interested in, so it was a great match, as far as Leo was concerned.

The wedding itself was to be a simple affair, followed by a meal at a pleasant restaurant in Haverfordwest, with a dozen guests. Leo was looking forward to meeting some of the people who worked with his mother at the Building Society, and some of Carl's fishermen colleagues. He felt annoyed with Gido for spoiling his good feeling. The prospect of the long summer vacation was clouded, now, by the possibility of the reappearance of the Dreamstealers.

Throughout the day at school, Gido's words kept coming back to Leo, and it began to dawn on him that, although he tried to set it aside as only a dream, he couldn't. Some corner of him knew that Gido had really been to see him, and that it wasn't a fantasy dream. He didn't want to think the visit would lead to anything more, or that Gido's cryptic message was serious but, inside himself, he knew it was. He tried to remember what Gido had actually said, and all he could remember was something about a brooch, and trouble in Dreamworld.

In a way, he would have preferred to forget it, but his thoughts kept going back to it.

'I wonder if Ginny's had any dreams,' he thought. 'P'raps, I'll text her and see.'

Then, he remembered that Ginny's gran, her mother's mother, had died only a few days before, and he thought he wouldn't bother her now. It wouldn't be a good time to introduce the topic of the Dreamstealers into her life. She was probably feeling bad enough already. Besides which, Leo had other things to think about. Everyone was talking excitedly about the coming weekend carnival in Narberth, which was where Leo lived. It was a once-a–year affair, a highlight in the calendar of everyone for miles around. People who lived as far away as Haverfordwest and Carmarthen made the trip each year, to join in the fun and festivities, and Leo was determined he would enjoy it.

This year would be special, because rather than going with his mother, Rhian, and his soon-to-be stepfather, Carl, he was deemed old enough to go with one or two friends.

After school, he and his friends, Greg and Lawrence (more commonly known as Loll), were standing by the school gates, talking about the coming carnival, when Bos Gribley, a boy whom Leo couldn't stand, walked past. Hearing their conversation, he stopped, turned to the little group and shouted,

'See youse lot tomorrer. Bets I've got more to spend than you 'ave.'

Smirking, he walked away. Bos was a bully and a sneak; he was also always rather broke, hard up, a cadger with never a penny of his own to spend.

'Bos's got money! I don't believe it,' Loll said.

'He can't have a job, can he?' asked Greg.

'Who'd give him a job?' Leo asked. 'No one round here would trust him as far as they could throw him!'

'P'raps he's nicked some money,' Loll said.

'Nah,' Greg said. 'He's lying. I bet he hasn't got any money at all.'

Leo, listening, remembered suddenly that, the last time he had met with Gido and his friends, they had warned him to be careful about Bos.

'He's been got at,' Gido had said.

A creepy feeling entered Leo when he recalled it. He had

thought no more about it until now, and perhaps it was only because of his morning dream that the memory had come back. If Bos had been 'got at' by the Stealers, he could be dangerous. It was a shock to Leo, to think he'd not observed Bos more closely.

The trouble was, he'd always disliked him, and it was easier to ignore him and steer clear of his company than to try to find out whether he was being, or had been, zombied by the Stealers. Even if he was, what could Leo do about it? Nothing.

He couldn't get it out of his mind though. He wondered what would happen if he and Ginny got pulled into another battle with the Stealers, like the one they had been in before.

The prospect was gloomy. He and Ginny, because they had certain special skills, had previously been picked out to rescue the Keepers. Neither of them really understood what these skills were, since proof of them seemed to have happened by accident. They had certainly been able to help the Keepers, who referred to them as 'psychic'. Ever since that time, Leo had been glad to feel that he was completely ordinary. Being psychic was too much trouble. He wanted to enjoy the school holidays, and get on with having a simple life, but something told that it was impossible.

Gido had sowed a seed and, in no time, it would grow into something real, he knew it. It was all a question of watching for the clues as they came, and if they did come, he was sure he would have no choice about following them. With a big sigh, he decided it was out of his hands.

He turned the corner into Picton Place, glancing up, as usual, at the grim ruin of Narberth Castle that stood on the mound behind. He stopped short, and stared at it.

The castle was lit by the golden rays of the lowering afternoon sun, and between the tall outlines of skeleton walls, he saw, like a watery reflection, three figures. One was a man in a frock coat, whose brilliantly coloured waistcoat seemed to pick up the rays of the sun. He was bald on the top of his head, but around his ears, long wisps of hair blew in the light breeze. This was Gido.

Beside him sat a round, little lady in a flowered apron, her dark hair scraped up into an odd, sideways knot on the top of her head. She looked like a cottage loaf. Leo knew she was Maria.

At her feet lay an animal, a creature whose face was human and would have inspired artists with its versatility and subtlety of expression. Its ears were cat-like, and though its fore-quarters were slender and smooth-haired, its rear end wore a bush of long, russet coloured hair. This was the one Leo knew as Grolchen.

Leo recognised them all immediately. They were the three Keepers. They were all looking at Leo as though they had been waiting for him to appear. Gido began to speak, and in Leo's ear, his words sounded like a stage whisper with static interference. It made him jump.

'It'll be a hot-bed of destructive anarchy until they actually have the brooch in their hands, unless you can do something. If I could do it myself, I would. I'd get down there and snatch it back, but it's on the outer circle, like this is. Hence the poor reception. We can be reached at The Way, in emergency. You know it, of course. What schoolboy doesn't know Carreg Coetan? Good luck with Cilgerran. If we can be there with you we will, but we may not make it. Choose your time – watch the moon and all that.'

The figures were dissolving and disappearing before Gido had finished speaking. Leo gazed at the spot where he'd seen them, convinced they would return.

He had no idea what The Way might be. He knew nothing of 'outer circles' and 'the moon and all that'. What did Gido mean about Carreg Coetan? Leo was not sure that he had heard of it. What on earth was Gido talking about? If Leo were going to get pulled into something, he would at least like to know what was going on.

He focussed on the mound, and tried to conjure them back by speaking to them.

'Where is The Way?' he said, out loud.

'No good asking a wall the way,' came a laughing voice from behind him. He turned with a start, and saw Carl approaching. He was on his way home from work. Feeling foolish, Leo grinned and said the first thing that came into his head. 'Learning my lines for a play,' he said.

'Thought you might be,' Carl smiled.

Leo wanted Carl to walk on home, and leave him to try to make himself heard by the three in the castle, but he realised he had no reason not to walk with Carl, who would think it very odd if Leo chose to stand in the street alone, talking to himself.

He glanced up at the castle, and Carl did the same. It stood empty; the shaft of light from the sun illuminated nothing more than the outline of the ruined walls against the sky. No Keepers reappeared.

'I never walk past it without looking at it,' Carl said.

'Me neither,' said Leo, and joined him in walking home.

He went to his room as soon as he arrived at the house, and tried to put down on paper as much as he could remember of what he had heard. It didn't make any more sense on the page than it did in his head, and the tantalising smell of supper, one of his mother's delicious chicken casseroles, wafting up the stairs, was doing a great job of distracting him. In the end, he screwed the notes he'd made into a small ball and threw it in the bin.

'How am I supposed to help them, if I don't know what Gido is talking about?' he asked himself. 'I'm just going to ignore them and, maybe, they'll go away and find someone else to do whatever it is they want doing.'

But he remembered that, on the previous occasion when they had needed help, the Keepers had been more than insistent about gaining his support, and he had an uneasy suspicion that the same thing was about to happen again.

Chapter 2

THE RETURN

GINNY HAD NEVER seen a dead person before. Her mother said she didn't have to go to the funeral, but Ginny had loved her gran, and, more to the point, she was curious.

Before the funeral, when she saw her at the Chapel of Rest, her gran looked just as though she was sleeping. Ginny stood beside the coffin, looking at the still face, with its familiar playful half-smile even in death. Beside her, her mother and her mother's twin sisters wept and murmured muffled goodbyes. Death is not so bad, Ginny found herself thinking. In fact, it looked rather peaceful. Aloud she said:

'I'm not afraid to die.'

'Good grief! Go on, outside with you! Whatever will you say next?' Her mother hustled her from the chapel.

Out on the sunlit street, Ginny could not hold in a smile that seemed to burst from somewhere low down in her body and erupt almost into laughter. Her gran was free! She was free from the horrible illness and free from worry. However, smiling was not what her mother wanted to see; and she told Ginny that unless she was prepared to look suitably sad at the funeral, she would not be allowed to go.

'I am sad, kind of,' said Ginny, 'but I'm sad for me, not for her.'

Her mother silenced her with a look, but Ginny saw Aunty

Bella wink at her from the back seat of the car, and she knew that at least someone understood her.

At the funeral, she sat between her mother and her Aunt Izzy. Aunty Bella was sitting with her latest boyfriend, in the pew behind them. She put her hand reassuringly on Ginny's shoulder when the hymns started, and Ginny knew that Aunty Bella had no idea of the words, just as she had none. Ginny had never been to a church service in her life, but Gran had, so they muddled through her favourite hymns, and the vicar said some kind words about her, and then they all knelt down on little cushioned stool things, and the vicar began to pray for her soul.

This was the moment when Ginny sensed something wrong. There was an unusual smell in the air around her; it reminded her of something, or somewhere, and made her uneasy. She screwed up her eyes, trying to keep them closed against the growing desire to look around. She tried to concentrate her thoughts on her gran, her friendly smile, her pointless stories, the way she complained about her age, the presents she brought Ginny at birthdays and Christmas, kindly intended gifts that were never quite right. It was no good. Her mind kept flying away, taunted by the smell in her nostrils, which made her feel a chill in her bones.

'What is it?' she thought. She lowered her head sideways and, with a tiny movement, tried to look behind, to see if Aunty Bella was praying with her eyes closed. Between Bella and her boyfriend, she saw, for a split second, as though in a bad dream come to life, two men sitting in the back pew. They wore dark suits, and, to anyone who knew no better, they could have come there with the undertakers. They were watching Ginny; she knew who they were, and she remembered, as though it had only happened the day before, when in fact over a year had passed since she had smelled it before, the gagging, putrid smell of the Stealers.

Ginny walked between her mother and Aunt Izzy, holding their hands, as they left the Church. Her fright had left her pale and shaking. Her mother, at last reassured by what she saw as a normal response to her gran's death, comforted Ginny and kept her close. Aunt Izzy gave her a mint and told her to be brave, and, the next thing she knew, they were back at home, and there was no sign of the two men, only the familiar faces of relatives and family friends around her.

Ginny helped to serve sandwiches, made pots of tea and poured glasses of sherry. She responded when kindly relatives spoke to her and said nice things about her gran, but she was not really there in the room with them at all. In her head, she was back in the time when her world had been turned upside down. She had thought it had gone forever.

For months afterwards, she had lived in dread, but nothing more had happened, and slowly she had begun to forget. Now, the memories were crowding in so fast that she could hardly believe she had pushed them away with such success, for so long. She thought herself a different person now than the one she had been then. She was taller and more confident. She no longer needed her glasses, except to read. Her short brown hair had grown longer and she wore it in a style that she liked to think made her look grown up. However, inside, she felt like a child again, when the memories started to come back.

When no one was looking, she drank a glass of sherry straight down, all in one gulp. It tasted sweet, like hot sun and raisins, and it made the bad feeling go away a little. So, she had another. Then she started giggling and fell over Basil, her dog, who lay sleeping on the kitchen floor. He was a small, sleek dachshund cross, grey in colour, and as slippery and soft as a seal. She cuddled him, sloppily planting kisses over him.

She and Basil had a special friendship. She walked him, fed him, and though she was careful that he shouldn't get overweight, she spoiled him with little treats whenever she could. When she tumbled over him and began her silly cuddling, Basil did not resist. He nestled close to her, giving her what comfort he could.

Then, for no reason, Ginny began laughing her head off and finally, she flopped into a chair, giggling and weeping all at the same time. Bella and her boyfriend carried her up to bed and Bella tucked her in.

'You alright pet?'

Ginny squinted up unhappily. The laughter had gone and tears pricked her eyeballs.

'It's Gran, isn't it?' enquired Bella, as though she already knew the answer. 'You were so brave this morning, but it doesn't do to bottle things up. You get a bit of shut-eye and you'll be fine.'

While she talked, Bella went to look at herself in the mirror on Ginny's dressing table. She straightened her short, tight skirt, pulled at strands of her mountainous, bleached hair-do and applied another layer of bright lipstick from her handbag. Her boyfriend was waiting outside the door.

'Do you want your mum?' Bella asked as she went to join him.

Ginny shook her head. How could she tell anyone what she knew? No one would believe her.

'Bella?' she asked in a small voice, 'could you ask Aunt Izzy to come up?'

She wondered why she had said it.

'Of course, darling. What a jolly good idea,' came Bella's reply as she left in a cloud of strong floral perfume.

Izzy came. Something about her made Ginny feel safe. She was not, and never had been, the good fun that Aunty Bella was and, more often than not, of the two of them, Ginny would rather be with Bella. Somehow, now, she knew that Izzy would listen to her and not laugh. Izzy sat on the bed and, for a little while, she said nothing.

Then she said:

'Your gran was quite mad, you know. A lovely woman she was, but completely potty.'

'Really?' For a moment, Ginny forgot her fear. This curious piece of information was not what she was expecting at all.

'Certainly,' Izzy continued. 'She couldn't tell us apart, Bella and me, when we were born, and so she called us both by the one name. We were interchangeable to her.'

'One name?' Ginny was intrigued.

'Isabella,' Izzy explained.

'Oh.'

'So, we were both Izzy and both Bella. She never could make out which of us was which. The only person who could tell us apart when we were little was Sara, your mum.'

Izzy laughed and tossed her straight, black hair back over her shoulders. She was wearing a dark suit with a pale blouse, and her face wore only a trace of make-up.

Ginny found herself smiling, when she looked at Izzy and thought of Bella's mountain of dyed hair, her micro skirts and her false eyelashes.

'No one would ever think you were twins now.'

'We found our way of handling it. There's usually a way of handling most things.' Ginny's mind went back to the two men. Izzy looked at her for a long moment, and then she asked, 'So, what's this all about? I thought you were very grown-up about your gran, especially in the Chapel of Rest, when you said you weren't afraid to die. Most of us are afraid of death, you know.'

'There's worse things than death,' Ginny blurted out.

Izzy's eyebrows rose. 'Go on, Ginny,' she said. 'Do you want to explain something to me, dear?'

'Aunt Izzy, please, if I tell you something, something that even Mum doesn't know about, will you...?' Ginny was unsure about how to continue.

Izzy waited, then, in the silence asked, 'Will I do what? Will I keep a secret? Will I believe you? You have to tell me what it is, first, darling.'

'I want just you to know, right?' Ginny continued nervously. 'In case anything happens to me. I want you to know.' Izzy nodded. Her calm kindness made Ginny feel surer of her ground.

'When I said there's worse things than death, I didn't used to know that, but it's true. When I was nine, I went to this stone circle in the Preselis. It's called Gors Fawr. Do you know where that is?' Ginny searched her aunt's face for reassurance.

Izzy nodded.

'I went with Dad and Rhian and Leo, her son. There was a stone there that fizzed when Leo and I touched it. Then, a man came up to us and started talking, and then Dad and Rhian disappeared with him. Leo and I went into the stone; and there were these people inside, who told us that the man was a Dreamstealer, and they said that he'd put them in there because they were rescuing people. This Stealer came after Leo and me, when we came out of the stone.'

Izzy put up her hand. 'Slow down. I'm sorry, Ginny. If you want me to understand you, you must explain a bit more. How did you get into the stone?'

Ginny frowned. 'We didn't know we were in it. We thought we were dreaming. We didn't really know what was going on. It was, well, you could say it was like getting into the middle of someone else's fight. And because we were there, these people in the stone – the Keepers they called themselves because they help people *keep* their dreams – asked us to help.'

'So, you helped, did you? What did you do for them?'

'We got them out of the stone. We rescued them, so that they could stop the Dreamstealers doing the horrible things they do.'

'What do they do?'

'They steal dreams.'

It sounded so small a thing that, even as she said it, Ginny realised that, without some kind of evidence of the full horror of their mission, she may not be taken seriously. Surprisingly, Izzy showed no sign of losing interest, or taking what Ginny said lightly.

'Go on. I'm intrigued.'

'See, now, how can I explain? They're not alive and they're not dead. They're in between. They came out of the Cauldron of the Undead.' Izzy's eyes widened but she said nothing, so Ginny carried on. 'Being undead is rather like being a zombie. They can't die, but they can't live either. So, they want everyone to suffer and to be like them. They want us all to be in a kind of greyness, as if we are dead while we're alive; and that's what happens when they steal the dreams. They throw them away and make people empty, so that all they want is money, and they can't feel anything good, or kind, or hopeful.'

'So you rescued the good guys?'

Ginny nodded. 'And we sent the Stealer back to Neptune, so he could die. So, in a way, we rescued him, as well as the Keepers.'

'I thought you said there was more than one of these Stealers.'

'There were three, but only one was the jailer of the Keepers, and he was the one that came after us. You can read about them, honestly. It's a very old story that is written down in a book of legends, and people think it's just a story, but it's true.'

Ginny's voice had become higher and more agitated as she spoke. She felt as though the more words she said, the less meaning they had, but Izzy was listening and showing real interest.

'I know the story of the Cauldron of the Undead,' she said.

'Do you?' Ginny was shocked and, for a moment, she couldn't believe it. 'So, you've heard about the Dreamstealers before?' Her breath was coming faster and her heart thumped.

'I've never heard them called that, but yes, I know the legend. I don't work in a library for nothing, you know. I do read books sometimes, and I have a special interest in myths and ancient tales.'

The bedroom door opened and Ginny's mother poked her head round it.

'Everything OK?'

'Yes, Mum.'

'It was very silly of you to go drinking sherry like that, Ginny, and I hope you've learned a lesson.' Her mother was cross.

'I'm sorry.'

'So you should be, after behaving like that at your gran's funeral, too.'

She was tut-tutting as she went downstairs. Izzy looked at Ginny, reached out, pushed back her hair gently and stroked her forehead.

'You poor kid,' she said. 'So, tell me why they chose you and Leo to rescue them, these Keepers.'

'They said, afterwards, that we were psychic, because we were the first people who heard them calling from the stone.'

'So, what made you suddenly decide to talk about it after all this time? It's such a strange story.'

Ginny heard something in her voice that she couldn't interpret. She had to know what was in her aunt's mind before she said anything more, and be certain that Izzy believed her.

'Do you think I'm mad, like my gran?' she asked.

Izzy shook her head. 'No,' she answered firmly, 'really, I don't think that.'

Ginny, reassured, leaned forward and whispered her fear into Izzy's ear, 'They were at the funeral. There were two of them and I know they're after me again. I bet they're outside here right now!'

'I'm sure they're not,' Izzy said. 'Would you like me to check?'

She smiled as she said it, as though they were playing a game, or as though it was all a bit of fun and, for a moment, Ginny wished she hadn't taken Izzy into her confidence. Izzy crossed the room and looked out of Ginny's bedroom window. She was able to see down onto one of Cardigan's busy, small-town streets below. She saw the tiny garden with its colourful display of early summer flowers. She saw the line of cars, indicating the presence at the house of all the guests. Further along, she could see the comings and goings of people from the video shop and the local convenience store. Two men in dark suits lounged against the railings of the Memorial Garden at the corner of the street.

'So, how do I know what I'm looking for? What do they look like?' she asked.

'They were in Church, at the back, in suits, like businessmen, kind of. The trouble is that they can look like anything they want to. They're not the same as us; they can change how they look. It all depends on things,' Ginny floundered.

'What things?'

'I'm not really sure. You see, I didn't really listen the last time, because I didn't understand. Leo listened and heard things about planets and stuff. but I was only nine. I'd listen now, I can tell you.'

'Planets?' Izzy straightened the curtain and returned to sit on the bed. 'Ginny, I want you to go to the window,' she said. 'Stand to the left and look down the street to the corner by the Memorial Garden.'

Ginny was out of bed and across the floor in a second and her face, as she turned back from the window, said it before her words.

'It's them.'

'I thought so. Now, what was it you were saying about planets?'

'I don't know. Honestly, I can't remember any of that. But it isn't important!'

'It might be.'

'It isn't!' Ginny cried. 'If a lion came charging up to eat you,

you wouldn't ask does it come from Africa, or India, or a zoo, and how did it get here? You'd just run and run! Only, I can't run and run. They've found out where I am, and there's two of them now, so it means that they've found out what we did, and they'll want to get Leo and me. I know it. I just know it.' She was hugging herself, becoming more and more upset.

'The only thing I know for sure is that they're scared of the sea,' she continued. 'They won't go near it. That's why I thought the other two would stay away. Cardigan's on the estuary, and Neptune could reach them, but they must be really desperate to get us, because they're here again.'

Izzy looked calmly at Ginny's anxious face.

'Those men came with the undertakers,' she said carefully. 'This tale of yours sounds very complicated, and I'm not sure where you got your ideas from.' She held up a hand and carried on speaking, when Ginny opened her mouth to protest. 'Listen. You've had a bad time in the last year or two. First, your dad walked out on you and set up home with someone else. Then, one of your dogs died, didn't he?'

Ginny nodded. 'Rolf,' she said. 'He was old, but I never thought he'd die.'

'Of course,' Izzy said, 'but he did, and now your gran's died, too.'

Ginny looked up at her, astonished. 'You think I'm making it all up don't you?'

'I think you're stressed, and when we're stressed, we get afraid of life, and fear makes us imagine things.'

'But you *saw* those men outside!'

'I did, and I saw them in the chapel at the Crematorium, but

I'm not sure they're who you think they are.'

'So why are they waiting out there?' Ginny demanded.

'I don't know. Maybe they're waiting for someone. What I do know is that you truly believe what you're telling me. So this…' She searched for a word. 'This adventure is real for you, and whatever I believe doesn't matter. I want to help.'

'You can't help,' breathed Ginny. 'I didn't tell you because I expected you to help. I just wanted you to know. '

'I think, more than anything, you need a holiday, a break from home, from…'

'A holiday?' Ginny echoed in confusion. 'But…'

Izzy raised an eyebrow. 'Okay. Let's say I believe you,' she said.

'But you don't,' Ginny growled, pulling the duvet up and burying herself as far as she could in it.

'We've got to get you out of here and away, and give ourselves some time to think,' Izzy said. 'I'm going to have a word with your mum. I'll tell her you're coming back with me, to my summer place, for a few days.'

'I can't go outside!' moaned Ginny. 'They'll see me.'

Izzy looked at her with real concern. Going through her head was the thought that her niece looked genuinely terrified, and was in a more advanced state of stress than she'd realised. Her only option was to play along with her until she could see how to handle it. She picked up a travel bag of Ginny's, which lay on top of the chest of drawers and, opening the drawers, began to fill it with clothes.

'Look,' she said, 'I'll get you out without them seeing you. While I'm downstairs, you get your mum's black hat and coat from her bedroom. I saw her throw them on the bed. Just grab them, put them on and join me in five minutes at the bottom of the stairs.'

'But...' Ginny emerged flushed from under the covers.

'What? Don't you want to come?'

'I do, but I want you to believe me, Aunt Izzy.'

'That's what I'm trying to do. You must admit, Ginny, it's a very weird story, and I need time to take it in.'

'But what will we do? Where will we go?'

'I'll tell you on the way,' Izzy said, disappearing downstairs.

Ginny went to her mother's room and put on the coat and hat, feeling very silly in them. She sat on the bed for five minutes, then, she followed Izzy down. As she came downstairs, she could hear her mother talking to Izzy.

'If you really think it would do her good, of course I agree. She has been looking a bit peaky lately. Did you make sure to pack some clean jeans, T-shirts?'

Izzy's voice, low and certain came floating up. 'She definitely needs a break, Sara. She's getting fact and fantasy mixed up. I went through something similar at her age, after Dad died, remember?'

Ginny nearly turned back. If Izzy hadn't believed a word she'd said, it was going to be difficult spending time with her, but what else could she do? She had to go through with it. Her mouth was dry at the thought of stepping out into the street.

'Stoop a bit,' Izzy whispered to her as they left the house. 'Try to walk like an old woman.'

So, Ginny, in her mother's long black coat and floppy hat, with a hanky to her face, stumbled down the path and into the waiting car, with Izzy holding her elbow.

'Every inch the grieving relative,' whispered Izzy as she closed the passenger door and strolled round to the driver's side.

The two men were still there, but their eyes were turned towards Ginny's bedroom window. It made her shiver. Izzy pulled away, without hurry, in the opposite direction.

'Maybe we should have a chat with Leo. Do you think he'll remember about this adventure you had?' Izzy asked, keeping her eyes on the road.

'Of course he'll remember,' Ginny flared, pulling off the hat. 'You think he'll say it never happened, don't you? And that it's all my imagination?'

Izzy ignored the question.

'Where are we going?' Ginny asked, as the car sped over the Cardigan Bridge and into Pembrokeshire.

'Down to Parrog, at Newport, darling; we'll be right by the sea, so you can forget about being afraid for a bit. Good place for a holiday don't you think?'

'I thought you lived in Aberystwyth,' Ginny said.

'I do,' Izzy replied, 'but Bella and I bought this house by the sea years ago. We thought we might live in it one day, in our old age. It's let to holidaymakers a lot of the time, but we always have a week or two for ourselves at the beginning of the summer, and I was planning to have a few days down there, so it's no trouble to take you with me. Now, why don't you just ring Leo and see if he can join us. My mobile's in my bag.'

Ginny tried his number. An answering machine crackled its message, so she left Izzy's number, trying to sound casual but urging him to ring back when he came in.

'Now,' Izzy said, 'relax. Stop thinking about it, and we'll wait to hear from Leo before we decide what to do.'

Ginny gave her a false smile. 'Okay,' she said, but she was unable to stop herself wondering how far behind the two men were and whether they had yet noticed that she'd disappeared.

Chapter 3

CLOSE RANGE

THE CARNIVAL WAS BRILLIANT. Leo had been to many others before, but none had been quite like this one. This, his first time without parents, had been unbeatable. He sauntered home in the dusk, humming as he walked. He had met up with Greg and Loll, as arranged, and spent the day with them. They had watched the procession of decorated trucks and floating tableaux, had joked and laughed, eaten hot dogs, ice cream and crisps, and drunk endless cans of coke. They had ridden on the waltzer and the dodgems; and played the Penny Falls, with little success. Finally, in the early evening, when their money had run out, they had gone their separate ways, with the sounds of music and fun fading behind them.

No wonder Leo hummed. It had been a great start to the long summer holidays. Only one incident had looked like spoiling the day, and a slight frown creased his forehead when he remembered it. A fight had broken out between Bos and Greg. Fortunately, it had stopped before it became serious; it was no more than a spat, but it had been unpleasant. Greg had been climbing on a handily placed wheelie-bin, from which he was about to stride across to a window ledge on an office building, to get a better view of the procession. He was poised mid-stride, when a sudden vicious kick at the bin had sent him hurtling to the ground.

Bos had been walking away, smirking over his shoulder, when

they picked up the dishevelled Greg, who was not badly hurt, but would obviously have some nasty bruises, and, for an awful moment, he looked as though he was going to cry. Instead, as the tears welled up in his eyes, he lunged through the gathering crowd, leapt at Bos, and succeeded in landing a fierce blow between his shoulder blades.

The heavy thump had knocked Bos off balance, and he crashed to the ground, with Greg on top of him, fists flying. All Leo could see were arms and legs writhing on the pavement. He and Loll, followed by several other boys, pushed their way through the crowds to watch the action. Thanks to the people around who had families with them, the fight was short-lived. A stocky man, with a child in a pushchair, grabbed Greg by the shoulders and pulled him away, whilst a large youth with his hair in a ponytail dragged Bos to his feet.

The two boys glared at each other. Leo, by this time, had made his way to Greg's side, and was in time to hear the man saying to him, 'You should be ashamed of yourself!'

'He started it!' muttered Greg, flushed and sheepish.

'I never,' Bos taunted. 'He just jumped on me, for nuthin'.'

Leo felt his hatred of Bos rising to hot anger. 'Liar!' he shouted.

Bos's looked away from Greg and stared straight at Leo. 'You? Useless geek, teacher's pet. You couldn't...'

Leo walked away, not interested in arguing with Bos. As he was walking home, he stopped and asked himself, what had Bos said, then? At the time, Leo had been so busy getting Greg away from the muttering parents and disgruntled crowd, he wasn't really listening, but now, he thought about those angry words spoken by Bos, and tried to recall them.

'I know he said something weird, something that made me jump inside. "You couldn't..." something...' he mused aloud. He racked his brains, but couldn't remember exactly what Bos had screamed at him.

When he arrived home, he let himself in. He enjoyed having the freedom of the house. It was a newfound independence, now that he was old enough to have no need of a sitter. Rhian and Carl were at a neighbour's barbecue, and had told him to join them if he wanted to. He didn't want to. He knew they would be home soon, but in the meantime, he could eat what he liked and watch what he wanted on the television. He did not register the flashing light of the answering machine.

He chose microwaveable chips and curried lamb from the freezer, and popped them into the microwave. Then, he channel-hopped, while he ate it. He forgot about trying to remember Bos's taunt. He was comfortable and easy in himself, thinking about nothing other than the pleasant prospect of the long school holiday ahead. Warm and full, he dozed lightly, after he'd finished eating.

'You couldn't fight to save your little sister.'

Bos's words flashed into his blank mind. He sat upright and repeated them to himself. Again, he had the same uncomfortable feeling that had swept through him when he first heard them. Bos did not know Ginny. Leo never talked to Bos. No one he knew talked to him, and he never referred to Ginny as his sister, but he knew that when Bos spoke about his 'little sister', he meant Ginny. He didn't know how he knew this, but he did. He broke out in a cold sweat.

'Oh, no! Oh, please, no!'

He struggled against the rising certainty that Bos's words, apparently so casually spoken, were a direct challenge, linked to the early morning visit paid to him by Gido. In sharp focus, he saw again Gido and the other two Keepers, Maria and the Grolchen, as he had seen them on that last occasion, by the stones at Gors Fawr, in the hills, warning him about Bos.

He grabbed his coat; he was out of the door and running back into town as fast as his legs would carry him. Bos was waiting for him on the fairground. The crowds of the day had drifted home, and now there were only clusters of youths and giggling girls, puffing on illicit cigarettes and eyeing each other. Leo strode through the gloomy shadows, in and out of the pools of yellow light around the sideshows and the hot dog stalls, looking for Bos, hating him, wanting him not to be there, but knowing he had to discover what his accusation had meant. He knew he would find him.

He was standing beside the rifle range, leaning against the brightly painted sign that said *Three Shots £1.00*. When he saw Leo, a nasty grin came to his face.

'You 'ad to come, din't yer?' he jeered.

Leo paused. His skin prickled all over and, for a moment, he almost turned back. Something was wrong here, something more than just a jibe from the school bully. He cleared his throat and stood, shoulders back, squarely facing his enemy.

'What did you mean about my sister?'

Bos shrugged. 'No idea,' he said.

Leo moved closer. 'What did you mean? Why did you say it?'

Bos's greasy mole–like face looked back at him as though he were speaking a foreign language, and, for a moment, Leo was tempted to hit him.

'Ask 'im,' said Bos, inclining his head toward the man behind the rifle range.

Leo turned. The man was cleaning a rifle, but he was looking back at Leo. He was tall and thin. So pale and thin, thought Leo, in that strange slow-motion moment, that he looked like a wand of paper. As the man with the rifle lifted his arm, his jacket opened, exposing white, gleaming ribs.

'It's a trap!' shouted Leo, panic rushing through him.

Too late, he threw up his hands to protect himself, as, with one swift movement, the man raised the rifle and fired it straight at him. Everything went black, and Leo crumpled and fell to the ground.

★   ★   ★

He fell from the sofa and landed on the floor, clutching his chest, gasping in terror and shivering from shock. The bang of the front door closing had coincided with the shot in the dream, and his mother's voice came to him through his half-awake state.

'You alright, love?' she called from the hallway. She and Carl had arrived home, entered the house and slammed the front door shut.

Leo tried to struggle to his feet, relief flooding through him. 'It was a dream, only a dream,' he whispered.

'Yeah, Mum, I'm fine. Dropped off to sleep and fell...' He raised himself to his feet, his heart hammering, and sat back on the sofa, his head in his hands. His mother went chattering past him as Carl came in behind her. Her words floated by, meaningless and unimportant. He struggled to calm the awful dread that still lay in the pit of his stomach. He heard Carl rewind the answering machine, then, the sound of Ginny's voice. Her halting message rang with a false note of cheerfulness, but only he seemed to detect it.

'Leo? Oh, I thought you might be in. I wanted to speak with you. Shall we do something special in the holidays? Er, can you ring me? Oh, yes, give my love to Dad and Rhian.' Then, she recited, slowly and clearly, a string of numbers, and then said, 'Er, Leo, it's important that you ring me very soon because I need to know.'

'She's a real little organiser,' said Carl, smiling, unaware of Ginny's hidden messages and failing to observe the tinge of anxiety in her voice. 'She'll want to know when the rehearsals for the kids' summer show are coming up, I expect, don't you, Rhian?'

Leo stood beside the answering machine, wishing that Carl would join Rhian in another room, and give him time to note down the numbers, to think about later, when he was in his room.

'Leo won't be in it this year,' said Rhian, returning from the kitchen, a glass of wine in her hand. 'He's too old. He's auditioning for the teenager's show in September, aren't you, love.'

He nodded but he was only half listening. He knew Ginny was in trouble, he knew what it was about, and he didn't want to know another thing. He wanted to go back half an hour, to the time when he had felt peaceful and comfortable, and had nothing to worry about. He knew he should ring her, but to do it now, and have the sort of conversation he expected, in the full view and hearing of Rhian and Carl, was going to be difficult.

He thought of going out to the public phone kiosk, but the

prospect of the dark street, with its possible hidden threats lurking in the shadows, brought a shudder of terror. The dream had been a warning. He knew it. He must ring Ginny and, if necessary, they would talk in code. Rhian and Carl had sat down and put on their slippers. Clearly, they did not intend to move for some time. Leo picked up the telephone and dialled Ginny's number. It was Izzy who answered, and she put Ginny on the line immediately.

Leo said, 'Got your message.'

Ginny asked if anyone else was in the room with Leo.

'Yes.'

'Oh! She paused, and then asked, 'Would you know what I mean if I said *they're back*?'

'Yes.'

'Leo, Aunt Izzy wants to know if you can come to stay with us at her holiday place.'

This was not what Leo was expecting. It threw him off balance, and he asked where this holiday place was.

'It's at Newport Sands, Parrog. It's right down beside the beach. *On the sea front. Get it?* Why don't you ask your mum and Carl if you can come?'

This was such a surprising turn of events that he wanted to think about it but, somehow, he knew there was no time to say, 'I might', or 'I might not', or 'What's it like?' He turned to see his mother and Carl cuddling on the sofa, laughing together about some silly shared joke.

Mastering his uncertainty, he asked, 'Mum, can I go and stay with Ginny and her aunt Izzy, at Parrog? She's invited Ginny and me to a have a holiday with her.'

He had no doubt that they would agree to it. They were more

than happy to see Leo off the next morning, on the first bus. They even helped him pack his bags, with what he felt was a bit too much enthusiasm.

'One of us would've given you a lift, but I need the car for work,' his mother said apologetically. 'Still, you'll enjoy the bus ride, won't you? Don't forget you have to change at Haverfordwest.'

Carl handed him two five-pound notes and told him to buy Ginny and her aunt an ice cream. His mother continued to issue instructions, and appeared to be almost as excited about him having a holiday as she thought he should be. He didn't feel excitement; if anything, it was apprehension, a cold fear that what was waiting for him was not going to provide a relaxing few days. He expected to face a fresh battle, with bad dreams thrown in. Still, he knew it was the only thing to do, and if it suited Rhian and Carl to have some time alone together, it also suited him to be able to talk to Ginny and find out what was going on.

'Just imagine, Leo,' Rhian said as he left the house, 'by the time you come back, the wedding will only be a week or so away. One bit of excitement after another!'

'Great,' he said, giving her a grown-up peck on the cheek, and resisting her arms, that were open and inviting him in for an emotional cuddle.

He took no notice of the other passengers on the bus, nor did he see the countryside sliding past outside the windows. The journey gave him time to think, and he determined to face what might be ahead with all his intelligence and with whatever psychic powers he could muster. The strong dream of Gido, followed by the one of Bos and the Stealer, had opened his eyes to the fact that he had again the ability to foresee danger, just as he had been able to foresee it in the past.

In his mind, he ran through once more the events that had sealed his fate as an enemy of the Dreamstealers. If there was one thing he had learned from that earlier encounter, it was that they were horribly dangerous, efficient at their chosen destructive path, and completely lacking in normal human feelings. They were outcasts from the human race. He knew they could come and go with ease between the material density of earth, and the subtle spaces of dream landscapes.

He knew from the stories he had read that they had not deliberately chosen to become what they were. It was Matholwch and the Cauldron of the Undead that had damaged them, had changed them into what they were, and had left the world with a problem that had remained unresolved for centuries. Even though he did not blame them for their condition, he could feel no real sympathy for them. The one Dreamstealer he had encountered in that earlier adventure, had scared him out of his wits.

How Bos fitted into the picture, Leo was not sure. He knew that the taunt that Bos had aimed at him in the dream was real enough, even though the dream was now fading, and he felt sure that the Stealers controlled Bos. Yet, he had no idea how they could have done it. He also wondered if there was any way in which he might contact the Keepers again. If Gido could come and go in Leo's half-dreams, then he should be able to get through to Gido, somehow, when he needed to ask for help. He must try to find out about 'The Way', though he had no idea where to start looking for it.

★ ★ ★

The bus station at Haverfordwest was crowded with people, boarding and alighting from the buses, and at the next bus stop, where Leo was to disembark and catch the bus for Newport, a number of holidaymakers was clustered, waiting to get on board. Leo struggled through the crowd with his bags, and went to the timetable, to check whether the bus that stood ready to depart was the one he wanted.

As he pushed his way along, he felt a hand on his jacket pocket, and he clutched at it wildly, turning about him to see who was touching him. He put his hand inside his pocket and felt around. Everything was still there: his bus ticket, his packet of mints, and his loose change. He counted the coins by touch. Nothing had gone at all. Then, he touched something in his pocket that he did not recognise, something stiff and with sharp corners. He pulled it out and saw that it was a picture postcard of Cilgerran Castle. There was nothing written on the back. He scanned around him, suddenly overcome with fear.

Who had put it there and why? Could it be one of 'them'? Had they, somehow, found out where he was going and were they lurking close by, watching him, waiting to do something terrible to him?

For a second, he sweated and shivered, then, he suddenly remembered that Gido had mentioned Cilgerran. He glanced around again, but no one in the crowd stood out as a possible suspect. As he calmed down, he realised that if a Stealer had dropped this in his pocket, he would surely have smelt its presence. Even though they could change their appearance, Leo knew that they could never be rid of the horrible stench, which the Keepers had said could only be smelled by a 'psychic', and that was why he and Ginny could identify them more readily than other people could. There was no waft of death in the smell of the people near him.

Perhaps, after all, this was a clue from the Keepers. He looked at it again, and tried to remember what Gido had actually said. It had been something about *'pulling in the parliament and taking Cilgerran'*.

He liked the picture of the castle. He was fond of castles and enjoyed visiting them, under normal circumstances, but he had a nasty feeling that visiting this one would bring more than just a peep at history and a picnic. He shoved the postcard back into his pocket. If the Keepers had sent this as a message, he should hold on to it. All clues, as he had learned on his previous meeting with them, had to be stored ready for the day when they would come in useful.

Ginny mentioned nothing about her fears, when she and Izzy welcomed him at the bus stop. They went straight to the house, a big, white-painted, semi-detached, built on a shelf of rock beside the water. Leo saw at once what a dream of a holiday place Parrog was. Izzy took him up to his room, which was on the first floor at the front of the house. Its windows faced out across the estuary, where small boats sailed back and forth, as though for his own entertainment. It was light, spacious and comfortable.

Leo dropped his bags beside the bed, and scanned the view with pleasure. This could be a great holiday if it weren't for the fact that he knew why Ginny had invited him. He'd expected her to show some sign of anxiety, but she hadn't. She had seemed fine, and he began to wonder whether he'd misinterpreted her call. Or, he wondered, was she afraid to speak in the presence of her aunt?

Izzy served lunch and while he ate, he looked at her out of the corner of his eye, and wondered how much Ginny had told her about the Dreamstealers. She appeared to be a very nice woman, kind and easy-going. She told Leo she was pleased to have him there as company for Ginny, and she fed them the most delicious food.

After they had finished the meal, Izzy suggested that Leo should help her with clearing the dishes, while Ginny walked down to the local shop to buy some more bread, which they would need for tea.

Once Ginny had gone, and they were together in the kitchen, Izzy turned to Leo, and, looking straight at him, she started talking calmly about the Dreamstealers.

'These characters,' she began, 'that sneak into people's dreams and steal their hope and goodness out of them; what do you know about them?'

Leo was shocked. He had not imagined that Izzy would come out with her question in that way. He shook his head and fumbled with a tea towel, not sure how to reply.

'Ginny's told me all about it,' Izzy continued, 'and I want you to know that I neither believe, nor disbelieve, what she's told me.'

Leo, who preferred to wait for her to continue, since he still didn't know what to say, greeted this statement in silence.

'I've come up against some weird things in my life,' Izzy said, 'not all of them logical or explainable. I'm prepared to accept that, whatever Ginny is going through, it is real for her, even if it isn't real in the sense that most people would understand the matter.'

Izzy seemed to be unflustered, but Leo knew it would be unwise to unburden himself, and tell her the whole story. No one else could understand what he and Ginny had gone through. Even this kind woman, if they tried to tell her the whole story, would say they were playing fantasy games, or imagining things. Izzy was expecting him to respond. She stood, hands on hips, smiling encouragement.

'We did have some funny things happen to us,' was all he could bring himself to say.

'Leo,' Izzy said, as they finished the dishes and she wiped the kitchen surfaces clean, 'I trust you to look after Ginny. How old are you now?'

'Nearly thirteen,' he said.

'Ginny's not eleven yet,' Izzy said, 'so you're old enough to help her understand that living in a fantasy world is no substitute for having real interests and real friends. I think she sees you as her friend. Don't you?'

'Well, yes,' he said. Izzy might be a favourite aunt, but Leo saw that she had not believed anything Ginny had told her. He shrugged his shoulders. What else had he expected?

'Good,' she smiled. 'I hope you're both going to have a good time here. Do as you please. Have fun. Go where you like, within reason, and keep her happy. Then, with luck, we can help her to put all this nonsense behind her.'

They heard Ginny coming back in. Izzy turned to Leo and said, 'What I really find amazing is where she acquired her knowledge of the myths tied up with this. I mean, where did she get it from?'

'Don't know,' Leo sighed, and smiled, as if he agreed with Izzy that Ginny was living a fantasy, but he was worried. He'd now taken responsibility for Ginny, and he knew that if anything went wrong, which it probably would, he'd be the one who was held to blame.

★   ★   ★

'What does Izzy do?' Leo asked Ginny, later, when they were seated on the sea wall, watching the holidaymakers, red and glistening from a day on the beach, making their way homeward for food and shade.

'She's the boss of the archives at the County Library.' Ginny paused and stared thoughtfully at the sparkling ocean. 'Leo, you're not cross about me telling her things, are you?'

'No,' said Leo. 'Just surprised that you did.'

'She knows about them, anyway, she says,' Ginny said. 'She reads lots of books about legends and myths. Anyway, she saw the two of them outside my house. They were watching my bedroom windows and I was so scared, I had to tell somebody. I'm not sure she believes me, but I told her it had all happened because we were psychic.'

'Yes, well, I still don't really know what being psychic actually means,' said Leo. 'Sometimes, I wish I'd never even heard the word. Are you sure it was them outside your house, and not just two men talking together?'

'Leo,' Ginny glared at him. 'I *smelled* them in church, at the funeral, and they followed me home. There were two of them, waiting, standing there, and just waiting.' She shuddered at the memory. 'What d'you think they want this time? It's not as though we've done anything like we did before, to bring them looking for us.'

Leo wished he had listened more carefully to what Gido had told him, and to the conversation on the mound.

He sighed and said, 'Look, Ginny, I guess we'll find out sooner or later. Right now, the only thing I know for sure is that they wouldn't be hanging around if there wasn't some bad reason, and, whatever it is, I am positive that it has something to do with Cilgerran Castle.'

He took the postcard from his pocket and showed it to her, and told her as much as he could remember of what Gido had said.

'I definitely don't want to go there!' Ginny exclaimed miserably, when he finished speaking. She wrapped her arms round herself and shivered, in spite of the warmth of the sun.

'I have a horrible feeling,' Leo said, 'that we won't have much choice.'

Chapter 4

THE OUTER CIRCLE

AFTER THREE DAYS at Parrog, Leo and Ginny had begun to feel they might have over-reacted to the threat of the Stealers' return. Nothing happened to fuel their initial fears, and they began to relax and enjoy themselves. Izzy was content to be in the background of their activities. She fed them well, pointed out on the local map places worth visiting, packed up sandwiches for picnics, washed and dried their swimming togs daily, and generally made sure they had exactly what she thought they were there for, a holiday break and a diversion for her distressed niece. The sun shone, the sea was lake-calm, the village people were friendly, and it looked as if the Stealers had been scared away by the children's proximity to the ocean.

But, on the fourth day, events took a sinister turn. As usual, Leo went out in the morning, to visit the local shop, pick up the morning paper for Izzy and to buy a pint of milk and a warm crusty loaf for their breakfast. He rose earlier than Ginny, who took ages to get ready to go out, and he set off alone and cheerful. On the way, a loud screeching and cawing caught his attention. He looked up and was amazed to see two huge crows attacking a passing seagull. In mid-air, they dive-bombed and pecked viciously at the gull, which turned and attacked the crows, in order to defend itself. The gull's enormous bill looked like a pair of huge yellow scissors. The bird was bigger, stronger and more dangerous than the crows, which obviously realised this and flew off. The gull, relieved of their attentions, flew out over the sea. The crows, Leo saw, had landed on a nearby telegraph wire. They continued to caw, a horrible harsh sound, and, for a disconcerting second, he could have sworn they were looking back at him, as he stared in their direction.

He shrugged and told himself off for thinking such rubbish, but, even so, it was odd that they should be there. Crows live in big groups and roost in trees. What were they doing, right down by the beach? He decided he would ask Izzy, when he got back, whether she had ever seen crows attacking seagulls near the sea. However, something happened then, which put the whole thing out of his mind. Mr and Mrs Hallett were from London and they owned a holiday house two doors down from Izzy. They had two daughters of roughly his and Ginny's ages, and whenever they met them outdoors, they would all smile and say hello. Leo was on his way back from the shop, when Mr Hallett, a big, broad man with a shock of fair hair and an open friendly face, hailed him from his front door.

'Like to come out for the day with us, Leo, you and Ginny?' he called. 'The girls would enjoy a bit of fresh company.'

Leo wasn't sure the prospect of being cooped up in a car with a bunch of girls and Mr and Mrs Hallett was such a great plan, but he wasn't sure how to say no. He and Ginny had nothing else planned for the day, and, as if it was already decided they should go, Izzy appeared on her front step at that moment, looking curious. When the request was repeated to her, she beamed.

'Lovely idea,' she said. 'It'll make a nice change for them.'

That was it. Less than an hour later, they were seated in the

Hallett's smart people-carrier and whizzing their way down the main coast road.

'First stop,' declared Mr Hallett brightly, 'The Iron Age Village.'

Leo thought that sounded okay, until Mr Hallett continued by announcing, 'Second stop, Cilgerran Castle.'

His words hung in the air. Leo felt cold, as though the temperature had suddenly dropped from the warm ambience of a summer's day to ice-cold draughts of danger. If anyone else felt a chill wind blow through the car, the only one to show it was Ginny. Leo looked at her and realised that she was less than happy.

'Cilgerran Castle?' Leo was trying to invent a reason for avoiding the place. 'I've heard that it's not worth the bother. I mean, I quite like castles, usually, but p'raps we could skip Cilgerran and go to a really good one, like Castell Coch, or Dynevor or somewhere?'

He realised he was being more than cheeky. The two Hallett girls stared at him. One of them started to giggle, but Mr Hallett didn't take it badly. He chuckled and began to tap the steering wheel with his left hand.

'Sorry to disappoint and all that, Leo, but I've set my heart on seeing Cilgerran, and there it is. Besides, I'm not planning to drive hundreds of miles to any other castles; I'm on holiday too, you know!' He said this with a laugh, in which his wife joined him, as though they were amused at Leo's suggestion, but not annoyed.

There was nothing to do but go where Mr Hallett said.

At that moment, no matter how hard he tried to avoid getting into danger, and taking Ginny along with him, everything would conspire to lead them into confrontation with the Stealers again, and Leo knew that he might as well throw up his hands and say, 'I give in.'

Leo tried to make the visit to the Iron Age Village last as long as he could, and it was only when an irritable Mr Hallett said, for the fourth time, 'Leo, the rest of us are ready to move. Come on, now! You've seen everything there is to see here,' that Leo conceded defeat and agreed to leave.

Back in the car, bowling along at speed, Leo tried not to think what lay ahead.

'You obviously like history,' Mr Hallett said to him. 'I've never seen a boy so interested in how pigs were kept and cooking was done in the Iron Age. Are you planning to be a historian, Leo?'

'Not in particular,' Leo said, wondering how to explain his weird behaviour. 'I do like finding out about the past though.'

'So, you'll enjoy Cilgerran Castle, then,' Mr Hallett continued, 'and no matter what you've heard, all castles are fascinating; big, small, ruins and entire, makes no odds to me. Mrs Hallett and Suzie and Carrie will tell you, I'm a fiend for a castle, I am, and it will probably be me that can't be dragged away from the place this time.'

He laughed, and his family laughed along with him in a dutiful way, as though they were used to his little jokes at his own expense.

'It's his metal detector,' Suzie, the elder sister, said. 'He takes it to every castle he can get to.'

'Some of them don't allow it,' Carrie said, 'but Dad takes no notice. He just does it when no one's looking.'

'I wouldn't break the law,' Mr Hallett said. 'I bend the rules, that's all. If I found anything of any value, I'd give it up as Crown Property – obviously.'

'Ha, ha,' Suzie said, in a sarcastic 'I don't believe it' kind of way.

'Oh, he would,' Mrs Hallett insisted. 'He's not a thief. He's an adventurer, a discoverer.'

'Why didn't you get your metal detector out when we were at the Iron Age Fort?' Leo asked.

'Too busy, too many people about,' Mr Hallett replied. 'Besides, it's debatable whether it's an original site, but castles – well, you never know what they might yield. You might like to have a go.'

'Thank you,' Leo responded politely.

'Ooh you *are* honoured!' Suzie said, and rolled her eyes as if she thought metal detecting was the most boring thing in the world.

'How about you, Ginny?' asked Mr Hallett. 'Would you like to have a go?'

'Maybe,' Ginny said. 'Is it difficult?'

Suzie was shaking her head, mouthing 'no, don't do it' and Ginny nearly laughed aloud.

'Not a bit, not a bit,' he said. 'I'll show you what to do.'

★　★　★

The village of Cilgerran seemed to be sleeping in the mid-day sun when they arrived. It was a gloriously hot July day, and they expected to see large numbers of people about. Instead, there was an almost eerie deadness to the main street. They parked in a lay-by, near a footpath with a sign that said 'To the Castle', and climbed out, looking around at the virtually empty street.

'Anyone for a bit of chocolate, or a lolly?' asked Mrs Hallett, spotting a general store nearby.

Carrie nudged Ginny as they walked to the shop. 'Look at that weirdo,' she muttered, nodding toward a man who rested in a reclining position against the wall of a house further along the road.

'He looks drunk,' Ginny said. As she spoke, the man looked up, straight at Ginny. He couldn't have heard her from that distance, she knew, and though she couldn't see his face clearly, what she did see were the two livid sparks of his eyes.

Her breath seemed to stop, as a stifling fear gripped her. Leo had gone ahead and had seen none of this.

By the time Ginny caught up with him, he was inside the shop with Mr Hallett, rummaging through some handbooks and tourist brochures, looking for information about the castle. Mrs Hallett was buying ice creams and sweets, and cheerfully chatting to the friendly shopkeeper.

'Might as well do some research,' Leo said, glancing at Ginny. He stopped short, seeing the look on her face. 'Where?' he asked, not needing to say more.

'Outside, on the pavement, playing a drunk,' she whispered.

Leo gritted his teeth. 'I knew,' he said. 'I just knew this would happen.'

'What shall we do?' Ginny's voice must have carried further than she realised because Mr Hallett turned to her.

'Do?' he asked, as though genuinely amazed. 'We walk down the path, and find the castle. That's what we've come for.'

Mrs Hallett was still firmly engaged in conversation with the man behind the counter, so they waited, and what they heard was not altogether comforting.

'You're quite right,' the man was saying. 'It is quiet, too quiet. We usually have a good flow of people through at this time of the year. I can't understand it. People seem to arrive, and then leave without getting out of their cars.'

'Why d'you think that is?' asked Mrs Hallett, breaking open a chocolate bar and looking as though she was set to talk for half an hour.

'Can't imagine,' said the man. 'It's odd. You didn't feel anything strange, when you arrived, did you?' She shook her head, munching cheerfully. 'Something is odd about the place, anyway. There's a funny mist that comes down over the castle in the evening,' the man continued. 'I've lived here all my life and I've never seen anything like it before.'

'Global warming, I expect,' Mrs Hallett said, as though she was the world's wisest environmental scientist. 'The weather's changing everywhere, all over the planet, doing the most peculiar things.'

The man looked at her curiously. 'You could be right,' he said, 'but it doesn't *feel* like it's anything to do with weather. Then, there's something peculiar about the birds.'

Leo's spirit was sinking. He kept thinking about Gido and his warning about having to save the castle. Leo didn't want to go there. It was the last place on earth he wanted to be, but he was aware that had no choice. Something outside his control was shaping events and forcing Ginny and him into danger.

Eventually, Mr Hallett edged his chatty wife out of the shop, and assembled them all outside. Armed with the metal detector, a picnic basket, two small booklets about the history of Cilgerran, which Leo had bought, and enough sweets to keep them going for a fortnight, they headed towards the path that led to the castle.

As they turned down from the road and onto the path, Leo sneaked a sideways look at the man who was lying on the street. He wasn't sure whether Ginny had got it right this time. The man was not watching them. He lay with eyes half-closed, an empty bottle in his hand, apparently an innocent drunk. Leo could detect no smell in his vicinity, which added to his feeling that Ginny was mistaken. Though the man was some distance away, he would have expected to get a whiff of something. It was always the first clue to the presence of a Stealer, for both Leo and Ginny. They had wondered at first why no one else could smell it and recognise it, but Gido had said that it was due to their unusual psychic talent.

'Just think,' Gido had said, 'how fortunate you are to know that smell and sense the danger, whereas others walk straight into awful traps, believing the lies.'

However, on this occasion, since there was no smell, Leo felt that, maybe, Ginny was imagining things. They followed the path, and, for a few moments, his spirits lifted, but not for long. He was a few paces behind the rest of the group, when he heard a movement behind him. Turning back, he saw the drunk standing at the end of the path, watching them. The smell, now contained between the walls on either side of the path, wafted strongly toward Leo on the breeze, and the man's eyes seemed to be boring holes into his skull.

'Oh no,' Leo let out a low moan; a mixture of fear and anger. He walked more quickly.

'Stay together,' he whispered, when he got close to Ginny. 'Stay with everybody else, all the time. Don't go off on your own, or get left by yourself. We'll have to hope that there's only one of them after us.'

'Two of them came to my Nan's funeral,' muttered Ginny. 'They're both here, I bet you anything.'

Mr Hallett marched ahead. He stopped to remove the metal detector from the black polythene bag in which he had hidden it. The lack of people around made him bold. Leo, watching him smiling in anticipation, suddenly feared for him. He knew that if Mr Hallett were not careful, a Stealer would take and change him. He had seen it happen before, and he had no desire to see it happen again. How could he be warned, or else be protected? Mr Hallett was a jolly sort of person, one of those people whose families love their oddness because they have other good qualities: kindness, understanding, and a good-natured way with others. Leo couldn't bear to think what he would be like if one of the stealers changed him.

Maybe, Leo thought, with a sense of dread, it would not be the husband, but sweet-natured, sweet-toothed Mrs Hallett, or one, or both, the two girls, that they would aim for, even though he and Ginny would be prime targets. It was deeply worrying; to think that he might be responsible for these people getting involved in a battle that was not theirs. Though Gido had told him it was everyone's battle, he didn't feel the Halletts would quite see it like that. He wanted to shout at the top of his voice, 'Let's go! Now!' but, of course, he couldn't, not without looking stupid, or opening himself to all sorts of unanswerable questions. So, he stayed silent, and kept watching furtively, to see whether the Stealer was following.

They walked together across the soft, green grass of the outer ward, towards the building itself. It was immense. Huge, dark towers and high stone walls loomed above them, a monumental tribute to those who had built the castle, centuries before. Parts of it were intact, others had crumbled into ruin. Signboards, everywhere around the perimeter, warned of dangerous drops to the deep gorge below them.

'Watch the signs,' shouted Mr Hallett. 'They're there for a reason. Don't do anything silly now, any of you.'

Leo and Ginny, huddling together behind the Halletts as though their lives depended on it, walked into the first tower. This was a large, round edifice; cold and damp, with weeping walls and a smell of must and decay, it made them shiver, after the warmth of the day outside. Steps to the left of the entrance ascended and curved around to the top, where an opening in the wall led to a walkway. This was built to allow tourists to roam around the top of the high walls.

'The view from up the top should be remarkable,' Mr Hallett said, walking toward them. 'Did you see how high up we are? How deep the gorge is below us? What a place!' He started to climb the steps, whistling cheerfully.

Leo sensed danger all around. He had no wish to climb to somewhere where he might feel an unexpected thrust from an unseen hand that would make him tumble off the tower and into oblivion. He had seen the gorge already. It was deep, dark and threatening; at the bottom, the river tumbled noisily over sharp rocks. As he hesitated, Leo noticed another set of steps, which went the opposite way, down into what had obviously been a dungeon. Neither route looked very appealing. Ginny shook her head sadly and stood closer to Leo.

The Hallett girls scurried up the steps, after their father. Obviously, they felt safe whilst they were near him, and, unaccountably, they showed no sign of wanting to wander off on their own. Perhaps, they also sensed that the almost empty castle held secrets that it would not be in their interest to find. Whatever the reason for their eagerness to be near him, they rushed to their father's side, and Mrs Hallett followed immediately behind them.

Leo and Ginny braced themselves. They knew that, for safety's sake, they should stick with the others, but they were keenly aware of the danger that was lurking somewhere close by. Suddenly, beneath them, low down on the flight of dark steps that descended to goodness knew where, they heard a sound. It was a mewling, pathetic, tiny noise, as though a small animal was trapped.

'It's a cat,' Ginny said, straining to hear better. 'Or a dog, maybe. Isn't it?'

They listened. The sound came again.

'I'm not sure,' Leo shook his head. 'We should stay with them, Ginny. It could be a trap, to separate us from the Halletts.' He indicated the upper steps and asked her to go ahead, but Ginny stayed put.

'It's crying,' she said obstinately. 'It's an animal, trapped somewhere. I'm sure of it.'

'Maybe it is,' Leo said, 'but it's not our job to rescue it. Not today.'

'We have to help.' She turned and looked at him angrily. 'You can't walk away when something sounds so frightened and so hurt.' The noise grew louder. 'I'm going down,' she announced.

Without looking back, she took off down the steps, into the

gloom, calling in a high, anxious, voice to whatever was in distress.

'It's alright. I'm coming to rescue you.'

The sound of her shoes on the cold stone echoed back to him. Leo heaved a huge sigh. It was no good; he had to follow. It occurred to him, vaguely, that the dungeon might be a more threatening place than the heights of the tower walkway, but he followed because he couldn't let Ginny out of his sight. At that moment, unable to do anything else and with no time to stop and assess the situation properly, he felt irritation with her for leading them on a wild goose chase.

When they arrived at the foot of the steps, it was almost impossible to see where the noise was coming from. Shadows lurked in every corner of what appeared to be endless dark chambers, linked by archways. Water dripped from the walls, making tiny, plopping sounds that echoed and confused their ears. They made their way cautiously forward, stepping on uneven flagstones, watchful for what may be ahead.

Leo was certain that it was all wrong to be there. He remembered how he had visited a dungeon at a castle with his father, when he was very small, and how, for weeks afterwards, it had given him nightmares about being trapped below ground.

'Don't go any further,' he commanded, and his voice sounded hollow and strange, bouncing back at him from the ancient stone.

Ginny stood obediently, arrested by the certainty in his voice, but she was also still listening, waiting for the cries to come again. Suddenly, from a corner, near to where she stood, and where her eyes, which were just becoming used to the dark, could see an untidy heap of old rags, the sounds of distress rose to an eerie wailing.

Leo did not see what Ginny saw, but he saw the effect it had on her, which was the exact opposite of what her reaction had been when she stood in the sun, on the surface. She screamed, and as the noise echoed around the tunnels, she turned and ran past Leo. She clattered up the steps as fast as her legs would carry her, with a startled, white face, eyes wide, breathing heavily.

Leo wondered what she had seen that he had not. For a moment, he hesitated. Perhaps, he should run, too, but his curiosity would not let him. He edged towards the heap of rags. Looking up at him from beneath the heap was a pair of eyes, which, as he tried to focus through the gloom, became a face. It was tear-stained, drenched in misery, bruised and desperate; and he recognised its owner.

This was the face of Bos Gribley, his enemy, but he did not look victorious or happy. He looked as though he was defeated and in despair. As he looked down at him, Leo, confused and dismayed by his find, heard a loud clanging noise behind him.

He turned fast and looked around. Behind him, where he could have sworn that there had been an open archway, there was now a heavy, studded door, and it was tightly shut.

Chapter 5

THE CASTLE

GINNY WAS GASPING by the time she reached the top of the tower steps; she stumbled onto the wooden walkway, which stretched in front of her; a rustic bridge joining the West to the East tower. The image of the face that had stared back at her in the dungeon was still vivid in her mind. She wasn't sure whether the eyes were those of a Stealer, but they certainly hadn't belonged to a tiny, trapped kitten, as she had first imagined. In her confusion, she could barely take in where she was, and, with deep breaths, she rested a moment, to calm herself.

Beyond where she stood, she saw the Hallett family clustered. Mrs Hallett stood slightly apart from the other Halletts. Across her feet was stretched a large, black bird, which appeared to be dying. Mrs Hallett was gazing down at it in disbelief, as were Mr Hallett and the girls, but from a slight distance. To Ginny, after the experience in the dungeon, this new discovery was suddenly terrifying. Mastering a surge of panic, she moved toward them carefully. The drop below, between the slats of wood, and to either side of her, was compelling to her eyes.

She heard Mr Hallett saying, 'Crow. He looks like a crow to me. But why? Where did he land from?' He looked up at the sky, as though he expected more crows to dive-bomb them at any moment. 'One second he wasn't there, and the next, well...' he continued, shuffling his feet uncomfortably.

Mrs Hallett was gazing fixedly at the bird. There was a trance-like expression on her face.

'He looked as though he did it on purpose,' Mr Hallett said. 'Didn't you think so, girls? As though he was aiming for something; obviously not your mother's feet, but something close. He seemed sort of intent.'

'Stop talking rot,' Mrs Hallett retorted sharply, as though she had suddenly come back to reality. 'Stop calling it 'he'. It's a bird, not a person.' She looked up at him briefly, reluctant to interrupt her vigil and take her eyes from those of the dying bird. The bird flapped its wings feebly. Her gaze was wrenched back to its hypnotic stare. 'Just stop calling it a he. It's an *it*.'

Mr Hallett frowned. He was unaccustomed to his wife being sharp. She was a gentle woman, kind, and not given to sniping at him over trifles.

'Sorry,' he said. 'It's just such a… well, such a big bird. But no, you're right. Fair enough. It could be either.'

'You just don't think,' she continued. 'You rattle on in that stupid way about everything we come across. What does it matter *where* it came from? Just move it. Move it from my feet! You're a man aren't you?'

Ginny felt real anxiety because Mrs Hallett had no idea what was happening to her, but Ginny knew. This wasn't just a bird, and Mr Hallett, though he didn't realise it, was quite right in identifying it as a male that had arrived deliberately. Ginny saw that Mrs Hallett had been lured into those deadly eyes, and now she was carrying on in a way that no one recognised.

'Pick the thing up and carry it down to the bottom,' she screamed at her husband. 'Save it, save it! I want it, and I hate it!'

This confusing information made Mr Hallett uncertain what to do next. He hesitated, then, seeing the look on his wife's face, he began unenthusiastically to roll up his sleeves. The bird was flapping, raising its large wings in spasms. Its eyes glowed bright yellow. There was a wildness in them, which Mr Hallett noted, even though they weren't turned toward him but were fixed steadfastly on his wife.

He saw the bird's suffering and felt a slight urge to help, if he could, but, equally, he reasoned that it might resist his attempt to grasp it. He had an odd feeling that the bird could read his mind and, as he moved toward it, he noticed its long, sharp bill, its claws and the powerful wings.

Ginny arrived beside Mrs Hallett and eyed the bird sideways, deliberately not looking directly at it.

'I wouldn't touch it,' Ginny said, addressing Mr Hallett. Her voice was low, but certain. Inside, she was shaking, but she spoke in a calm voice, and concealed her fear better than she'd hoped.

The Halletts looked, as one, toward her. Mr Hallett drew back. There was a pause as they took in her words, and Ginny realised they were waiting for her to say more.

Mustering all her courage she pointed at the dying bird.

'I think Mrs Hallett should just pull her feet out from underneath it,' she said. 'It isn't *that* heavy. Just heave it off. Step back. Someone could hold you steady, you know, hold your hand. Here, let me.'

She walked closer and offered her own trembling hand but Mrs Hallett ignored it. She looked furious. Her normally placid features darkened into a disgusted frown.

'What? Do you expect me to leave the creature here? Dying?'

'Yes,' Ginny said.

For a second, she caught sight of the bird's eyes as they swivelled in the direction of her voice. She lowered her head, and looked away and down. Seen between the narrow planks beneath her feet, the distant ground pulled dizzily at her, but she would not look up and into those evil, compelling eyes. She knew them only too well. Those were the eyes of a Dreamstealer into which Mrs Hallett was gazing, which were hypnotising her. She was not the same Mrs Hallett any more. Ginny was sure of it; and she was aware that if any of the rest of them looked into those eyes, they, too, might be caught.

She knew, from her own experience, that the first piercing gaze of the Stealer locked the victim in. It made them swoon, mirroring their own perfect innocent dreams, but in seconds, it left them empty, so that nothing could ever satisfy them again. Unfortunately, she saw that it would be difficult to say, 'Don't look in that crow's eyes. It will change you for life,' but she could think of no way to persuade Mrs Hallett to move, nor could she think of any way of expressing her fear, without the whole family thinking her mad.

The girls, Suzie and Carrie, saved her. They had been watching what was happening, had noticed the look on Ginny's face at the sight of the bird, and seen the way her eyes had dipped from its gaze. They were intuitively aware of her fear, and it made them courageous, though they had no idea why. A sudden, subconscious need to protect their family reared up inside them and, with a nod between them, they got behind Mrs Hallett and, each grasping an elbow, lifted their mother backwards. The evil bird rolled off her feet and onto the ground, its wings flapping feebly.

'Stop messing about, Mum,' Suzie said, as they yanked the

startled Mrs Hallett from where she stood.

'We don't want to hang about here,' Carrie said. 'Leave the bird. Let somebody else clean it up. They should have someone who does that. Birds probably die all the time.'

The bird let out a loud 'Caw', which shook Ginny, but seemed not to upset the girls at all. It was all done so quickly that Mrs Hallett didn't know what to think.

'That was stupid,' she shouted. 'Didn't you hear it cry? It hasn't finished!'

'Finished? Finished what?' Mr Hallett asked in bewilderment. 'What are you talking about?'

'Stupid, stupid, stupid,' Mrs Hallett was yelling, still trying to catch the bird's eyes.

'Stop staring at it, Mrs. Hallett' Ginny said.

'Quite right,' said a voice from behind her. In the shadows at the top of the tower steps was a figure. Ginny turned. She could not see the face of the person who stood there. She could tell from the shape only that it was a man, no more, but the voice was one she recognised.

'Gido?'

'Throw the bird over the rail and see what happens,' the voice answered. 'Don't look at him. I don't need to tell you that, Ginny, do I?'

Ginny's mouth went dry. If Gido, whom she knew as a friend, but who was hovering like a ghost at the top of the steps, wanted her to throw the bird down, then she should surely do it, but the last thing she wanted was to put her hands near that deadly creature.

'Couldn't you do it?' she called.

However, he was gone. He seemed to dissolve into the shadows and simply disappear. She turned back to the Halletts. Mr Hallett and the girls were already walking along the walkway toward the far tower, talking amongst themselves, as though the incident had been nothing more than a peculiar diversion. Ginny realised she was the only one who had heard the voice from behind, and seen the shadowy figure. Mr Hallett's voice reached Ginny as she stood and wondered whether any of it was real, or whether the whole thing was a dream.

'Funny though, I could swear he was a *he!*' he was saying to the girls. 'Can't tell you how I knew, but I did.'

Mrs Hallett had not moved. She stood, red-faced with annoyance, pointing a finger at Ginny.

'How *dare* you? You're to blame for this poor...'

Before she could say anything more, Ginny leapt toward her. Mrs Hallett jumped back, thinking Ginny was about to push, or hit, her. Instead, Ginny bent swiftly down to the bird, which lay nearby. It twitched and flapped. Ginny looked away, avoiding the bird's eyes, shot out her arm, and grabbed it by its legs. It struggled, and one of its claws scratched her wrist, but Ginny had its legs closed tight in her hand, and she swung it high and threw it as far as she could. She put all her strength into the throw, so that where the creature fell, on the rocky ground beneath, would be as far from her as possible.

She watched it as it arced in the air, because, whatever Gido's reason for appearing, he had come to tell her something she knew was important. Half way through its fall, the bird hovered, spread wide its powerful wings, and, showing no signs of damage, it beat the air and turned full circle. Then, in a gentle swoop, it dived and disappeared, but it didn't land.

Ginny blinked. She knew she should have seen it make contact with the ground below, or rise up again. She looked up and around, wondering whether it had flown away. On the outer castle wall she saw a row of crows; they seemed to be observing her. Like a rapt audience, they did not move, but kept all their heads cocked at the same angle. Ginny shivered.

Mr Hallett called to his wife from the far tower. 'Come on now, dear. I'll help you down these steps. They're frightful; so steep and narrow.'

Mrs Hallett put her hand to her head and said quietly, 'I have such a terrible headache,' and, as though she had forgotten the bird and Ginny's behaviour, she called to Mr Hallett in a sharp, accusing voice, 'Why are you going without me? Just wait for me, will you?'

'I *told* you, my dear,' he called. 'I am waiting for you.'

Mrs Hallett walked towards the far tower and her family, leaving Ginny gazing down from the parapet. A man was walking below. He wore a long dark coat, his hair was white and wild and blowing about in the wind. For a moment, Ginny wondered whether it was Gido, but then the man turned and looked up. She shrank back. The face she saw gazing up out of that wild, white halo of hair was enough to tell her who it was.

'How...?' she breathed. 'How did he do that?'

The Halletts had gone out of sight, and she was completely alone. Her eyes turned toward the outer wall. Almost all the crows were flying away, but one landed again, and remained with its head cocked in her direction. She wondered if it was the Dreamstealer in one of his many guises, and if he were watching her. She put her head up and walked to the far tower, trying to stay calm and not to make a mad dash, convinced she was being observed. She was scared stiff on the inside, but there was no way that she would let the Stealer would see it.

'What's going on, and where's Leo?' she muttered, as soon as she was within the tower walls and warily treading the steps that led to the bottom. As she emerged out onto the grass, she looked cautiously each way, in case the Stealer, in bird or man form, was waiting for her. It was inevitable that one or other of the Stealers would show up, and she had no idea what to do next. Her greatest fears were that both of them would arrive at the same time, or the one she thought she had spied in the dungeon had actually got hold of Leo. She looked around for Leo, but there was no sign of him. If he had not got out behind her, he might be in very deep trouble.

Mr Hallett was poking his metal-detector in amongst a pile of rubble. He smiled in a friendly way at Ginny when he saw her.

'Thought I'd get my hand in,' he said. 'Last year, I found an early Roman coin. Not worth anything, of course,' he added hastily, 'only to an amateur collector like me.'

Ginny watched. In the background somewhere, she could hear Mrs Hallett shouting at the girls. Mr Hallett heard it, too, and Ginny could see he looked puzzled by it.

'Having fun?' he asked Ginny, to cover his confusion.

'Oh? Yes… yes, of course, thank you,' Ginny answered, and turned away, wondering where she would be safest. Should she stay beside Mr Hallett? Should she try to find Leo? She knew she should look for Leo, but the idea of returning to the dungeon was too difficult to think about, but then, she had an idea.

'Mr Hallett,' she said.

'Call me Jimbo,' Mr Hallett said. 'Everybody does.'

'Jimbo,' Ginny began again, 'in the dungeon, where I went before, I could swear there was something sort of *glinting* in the ground. It was just here and there. I mean, I didn't look properly. It's a bit spooky down there, but I don't suppose many people go in and explore, do they?'

'Are you asking to borrow my detector?' he asked, looking pleased. 'No one can resist it for long. It's just so fascinating, isn't it? I'll show you how to use it.' He began twiddling little knobs and switches on the handle. 'Watch now, and I'll explain how to find things with it,' he said.

'No,' Ginny replied hastily. 'I'd much rather watch you use it. I'm hopeless with things; always breaking them.'

'Really?' he looked surprised. 'It's very honest of you to say so. That means you don't want to use it; is that right?'

'No, but I thought you might find the dungeon interesting. I'll show you.'

Mr Hallett shrugged. 'Lead on,' he said. 'It can't be an actual dungeon. There are no dungeons here. I've looked at the plan on the notice board. What made you think it was a dungeon?'

'Because it's below the ground,' Ginny said, as they walked back across the wide grassy slope towards the tower, 'and that's where dungeons were, weren't they?'

Mr Hallett nodded agreement. 'But,' he added, 'I have to say, that it is the last place in the world where there's likely to be anything valuable!'

They reached the tower, and, as soon as they entered, Ginny froze. Where the steps to the dungeon had led downward was only a dusty area of floor, made of unbroken concrete.

'The steps! They were here!' Ginny cried.

Mr Hallett cast around the circular wall of the tower, in case she had the wrong spot, but his search yielded nothing. There was no entrance to a lower flight of steps anywhere.

'Funny, that is.' Mr Hallett scratched his head. 'Come to think, I'm sure I saw some steps, too, when we came in before. I didn't think much about them at the time, but there was a sort of dark corner that looked quite like the start of some steps.'

He pointed to the corner where Ginny knew they had been. 'There,' he said, 'right below the steps going up the tower. Obvious, isn't it. That's where they would have been, but they're certainly not there now. Weird, that is.'

'But you *thought* you saw them?' asked Ginny.

Mr Hallett shook his head. 'Couldn't have done, could I?' he said. 'There are no steps, Ginny. We were mistaken.'

'Try your metal detector there,' Ginny prompted. 'It may be something that might...'

'Now listen, young lady,' Mr Hallett interrupted her, obviously not pleased, 'You told me you'd been into the dungeon. Why did you tell me that, eh? Why did you tell me a fib like that?'

While he waited for Ginny's response, he couldn't resist waving his metal detector around the area. Before she had time to think of a reply, a gust of wind blew through the tower. The weather outside was still and calm but, out of nowhere, a whirling wind spun and buffeted the internal walls. Ginny found herself pinned by it, unable to move, watching in astonishment as Mr Hallett's outstretched arms were lifted high into the air.

The metal detector dropped from his hands, and the blast hurled it across to the wall at the far side of the tower. Ginny felt the wind blow round her. It was so warm; it felt as though it had come from the Sahara Desert. It felt like a good wind, not an unfriendly one, and though there was no one to be seen, Ginny sensed, once again, the presence of Gido. Why he should choose to make such a wind blow Jimbo's toy from his hands, she couldn't imagine. The wind soon dropped to a gentle breeze, swirling the dust on the floor into strange shapes and patterns.

'Well! Good grief! Whatever next?' Mr Hallett grumbled as he went to retrieve his precious metal detector. He stopped abruptly, and his eyes popped.

'Look!' he cried, pointing. 'It's going crazy.'

Ginny joined him and saw he was right. The instrument was turning itself round in circles, crackling and twitching like a live snake.

'I've never seen it do anything like that before,' Mr Hallett said.

He tried to reach out and grab it, but each time his hand came near it, the thing moved again. It seemed to be scraping away at the covering of dust and earth, and, suddenly, Ginny saw something glisten at her feet. She reached out and grabbed at it.

The moment she picked up the round metal object, the wind died completely, and the detector lay still.

'What is it?' Mr Hallett asked, peering at Ginny's clenched hand.

She unclenched her fingers and showed him. In the palm of her hand, there lay something that looked like an old tin lid. It had a rough, jagged, circular edge, as though it had been cut by a tin opener, and pressed into it was some lettering and numbering, like a sell-by date. Mr Hallett took it, turned it over, examined it, and even put it between his teeth and bit it but he was finding it hard to concentrate, for some reason. The weird wind, the strange behaviour of the metal detector, and the disappearance of the lower steps had spooked him more than he would have liked to admit. Ginny could see beads of perspiration on his face.

He bent to pick up his metal detector, now lying inert and innocent on the ground, and passed the tin lid back to Ginny.

'Top off a baby food can, by the look of it.' He shrugged and started to walk outside again, making for the open air and normality. 'You'd think people would be a bit more careful about their litter, wouldn't you.'

Ginny ran after him, holding out the tin lid, offering it to him. It was, after all, his treasure.

He shook his head. 'Keep it,' he said, 'or throw it away. It's worthless.'

Ginny knew that he was wrong. She stuffed the lid into her pocket, and went back to the corner where the steps to the dungeon had been. Feeling silly, wondering if any of the Halletts could see, or hear, what she was doing, she stooped and began to whisper at the floor.

'Leo, can you hear me?'

Nothing. Once again, she tried, her voice a little louder this time.

'Leo, Leo it's me. Are you down there?'

Again, there was no reply.

Chapter 6

FRIEND OR FOE

WHEN LEO HAD first seen Bos's startled, tearful face peering out at him from beneath the pile of old sacks, his whole body had tensed, preparing to spring into a fight. Here was his known enemy and, in Leo's mind at least, an accomplice to the Stealers.

However, Bos's evident distress alarmed Leo, and, because it was not in his nature to kick a person when they were already down, he stepped back and asked,

'What's up, Bos? What're you doing here?'

'It was a man, a friend o' mine,' Bos snivelled. 'He told me to meet 'im at the castle and said 'e'd give me some money. Then, he shoved me down the steps, and locked the door.'

'There was no door here, when we came down,' Leo said, looking round at the strong door that now blocked their escape. 'Anyway, what did he tell you he was he giving you money for?'

'Nuthin',' Bos said, 'and there *was* a door, that's why I couldn't believe it when you and that girl appeared. I tell you, there *was* a door, and it was locked, like it is now.'

'People don't give you money for nothing,' Leo answered.

'*He* does,' Bos replied. 'He's given me loads, just for talking to him.'

'What about?'

'Mind your own stinkin' business,' Bos said.

Leo turned and looked at the door. 'Have you tried to

open it?'

'Course I 'ave,' replied Bos, as though Leo was an idiot.

Leo was watching Bos's eyes, and he saw them flicker sideways as he spoke.

'You haven't, have you?' he said. 'What a wimp! You were just lying here and crying.'

Leo ran up the steps to the door. There was a black iron handle on it, but no keyhole for a lock. He pulled at the handle, which was immovable. He stood looking at it. Bos raised himself up on his elbows, to see what he was doing. The door was made of thick planks, dull varnished, faded almost to the colour of stone. If you looked at it long enough, Leo thought, you could think it was part of the wall. He put his hand to it and touched it, letting his fingers move across its surface.

'It's not wood,' he said finally, 'it's not a door, either, and it's all stone. It's part of the wall!'

'What? Don't be a moron,' Bos said.

'I'm serious,' Leo said, beginning to panic. 'This isn't a door, Bos. There's no way out. We're walled in.'

Leo's knees felt as if they had turned to jelly. The growing panic swept through him, just as it had when he was little, and he'd had bad dreams of this very thing. He resisted it as strongly as he was able. He leaned on the wall and thought about the situation calmly. He was no longer five years old. He was nearly thirteen, and he had a good idea that, if the Stealers had intended him to be locked in here, there was probably even worse to come. It was important to keep his head, and to show Bos he was not afraid.

'No way out, Bos,' he repeated.

Bos did not reply. Leo climbed down the steps and began

looking carefully at the walls.

'It's dark in here, but not pitch black,' he said, 'but I can't tell where the light's coming from, and the air is kind of fresher than you'd expect, isn't it?' He did his best to sound optimistic, as much to lift his own spirits as to cheer the downcast Bos, who had slumped down again, and was leaning against the wall, looking miserable and defeated.

'I knew something 'orrible would 'appen to me,' he groaned. 'No one likes me. You don't like me, do yer?'

'Don't be so wet!' Leo yelled at him. 'What's that got to do with anything? Start looking for a way out, like I am. Don't just give up.'

'S'no good,' wailed Bos. 'We'll die 'ere. I know it.'

Leo gritted his teeth. He felt like punching Bos, on two counts; one, for getting him down there in the first place; and two, for being such a useless, cowardly person to get stuck with.

Bos continued to whine. 'If I die, no one'll care, so no one'll bother to come and rescue me.'

'Shut up,' Leo shouted. 'Just shut up. You're not making things any better by moaning about them. Besides, I'm here as well, and people *will* come looking if I don't get out.'

'Oh, lucky you,' Bos sneered sarcastically. 'You think you're so good because you've got friends and I 'aven't.'

'I thought you said this man who gave you money was your friend,' Leo said.

Bos said nothing. Leo peered into Bos's face. Despite the lack of clear light, he saw that the tears on Bos's cheeks were real ones, and that he did look genuinely terrified and distressed.

'Who was he?' Leo asked, trying to bring a little friendliness into the tone of his voice. 'Tell me his name.'

A sound behind him, somewhere beyond one of the arches that led into blackness, made him stiffen. He remembered with a jolt the dream that had caused him to topple from the sofa, the dream in which Bos had led him into a trap, and a Stealer shot him. His mouth went dry. He knew exactly who Bos's friend was. Now, in the murky recesses of the cold stone tunnels, which stretched away into blackness, that 'friend' lurked and awaited his moment to attack.

'Don't know 'is name,' muttered Bos.

'You must call him something.' Leo said, trying to talk as normally as possible, keeping an ear open for any more sounds of movement.

'Why?' asked Bos. 'Why should I? 'E just turned up one afternoon, when I was down the river path, and started talkin'. Then 'e said I could be useful to 'im, and 'e'd give me money for 'elpin' 'im out. That's it. That's all I know.'

The shuffling, scuffling sound reached Leo's ears again. Or, he wondered, was it his temples that were picking up the warning sound? He put his fingers to the points on the side of his face where he had been told his 'psychic ears' were sited. They were twitching. His chest tightened and he could hear the thud of his heart.

'Can you hear someone moving about?' he asked Bos quietly.

Bos raised his face and listened, then shook his head. 'Maybe you 'eard rats,' he said, hugging himself with fright. 'I'll bet there's enormous ones down 'ere.'

He started to cry again, making a soft whimpering sound like that which had first brought Ginny, and then Leo, to the rescue of what they thought might be a trapped animal. A wave of sympathy went through Leo, but he struggled with it.

On the one hand, he felt a sudden terrible pity for Bos, who, in his loneliness, was prepared to talk to, and accept money from, a total stranger, unaware of the dire consequences of his thoughtless behaviour, and who was now so scared he couldn't think. On the other hand, if Bos really had become an agent of the Stealers, and was deliberately playing a game of enticement to catch him, Leo knew he should stay on his guard. He was also becoming more apprehensive as the noises from the tunnel increased. If he came under attack here, where the Stealer had him in an enclosed space, no one could save him.

'You do know something,' he said, and his voice, to his own ears, sounded unsteady, but he ploughed on. 'You're a liar, aren't you. Bos? Look at how you lied when you started that fight with Greg, and how you're always lying about where you've been and what you've got. I mean, if you were in my shoes, would you believe...' But his words came to an abrupt halt, when the sound from the tunnel grow much louder.

He spun round. A loud shuffling of feet, magnified by the echo in the tunnel, sounded as though whoever was approaching was on the point of appearing. Leo leapt swiftly to the side of the arched tunnel entrance, and pressed himself flat against the wall. Bos stopped crying abruptly. Mouth and eyes wide, he clutched the rags around him and held his breath. Then, Leo heard something more than footsteps – a strange humming. In a moment of swift relief, he recognised it.

Stepping out of the entrance, he turned to look down the tunnel, and stared into a round, pink, human-looking face flanked by a pair of cat-like ears.

'Grolchen!' he cried.

'Mic,' replied the creature, but even as he spoke, he seemed to be fading away. He turned, waved his hairy rear-end and, with a back foot, beckoned to Leo to follow.

Then, he disappeared completely, not back into the tunnel, just into thin air. Leo blinked. Had he really seen what he thought he'd seen? Was it an apparition, a ghost, perhaps?

'Did you see that?' he asked Bos.

If Bos's hair had been long enough to stand on end, it would have. His face was a picture of dazed disbelief. 'What was *that*?' he asked, terror in his voice.

'You saw him!' Leo said, relieved. 'Thank goodness for that. I thought I might be going mental. *That* was a Grolchen. I know him, and he's definitely on our side. He must be having difficulty getting through to us. I've never seen him disappear like that before.'

Leo suddenly remembered the overheard conversation between Maria and Gido about Cilgerran Castle.

'It's on the outer circle,' he said aloud, as the words came back to him.

'What you on about?' grumbled Bos, getting up. 'That thing scared me 'alf to death. If that's on our side, I wun't like to see the enemy.'

Leo looked at him. He wanted to shout at him, 'You stupid idiot! The enemy just looks like a man who gives you money for being selfish and greedy!' But he didn't say it, because he knew that it was more important to get out than it was to start an argument. He pointed into the dark tunnel.

'I'm going that way,' he said. 'I think there's light coming from somewhere along there, and I'm sure that's the way Grolchen wanted me to go, judging from the way he crooked his leg at me, and he said "Mic".'

'Oh, and that means som'at, does it?' Bos said. 'Well, I'm not goin' down no dark passage because some weird animal says so.'

He ran up the steps toward the door and began to bang on it. 'Let us out,' he yelled. 'There's rats and animals and things down 'ere. Someone let us out.'

However, he only succeeded in hurting his fists, and he soon realised that Leo had been correct in thinking they were walled in. What looked like a door was not a door. It was stone, and the iron handle neither turned, nor moved under his hand.

He started to swear, and cry again, and Leo, exasperated by him said, 'Grolchens have only three words: there's Mic, which means everything good and positive; Gek, which means the opposite; and, well, there is one other word, but it's their swear word, and I'm not allowed to repeat it.'

Bos was looking at him as though he was mad.

'Anyway, I heard him say Mic, so I'm going,' Leo said. 'It's worth a try. There may be a way out down there.'

He had come to the conclusion that, if the Stealers had set up the trap in the dungeon, they would return to release Bos if he was working for them. If he wasn't, then Leo might be making an unkind mistake by leaving Bos alone in the dungeon again. Leo knew he had to do something, and that the Grolchen had not appeared for nothing. He had brought a message, and the message was that Leo should follow him, and so, he did. He walked through the archway without looking back, but then he found himself stuck, unable to go forward.

'I can't do it,' he whispered to himself. 'I can't leave him there on his own.'

As he was about to return to Bos, he could hear Bos entering the passage, hurrying to catch up with him.

'You pig-faced rotter,' screamed Bos. 'You'd leave me on my own.' His voice echoed through the blackness, coming back to them, loud and angry, '...*on my own... on my own.*'

'I'm still here,' Leo said, right beside him. 'See.'

This shocked Bos into silence, but not for long.

'I can't see anythin',' he called, more careful of the sound of his voice, but even his whispering came back to him magnified '...*anythin' ...anythin'.*'

'It's like an echo chamber,' Leo said, moving forward, and hearing his own voice rumbling around him. 'Stay close to the wall. That's what I'm doing. It's a bit wet, but if you hold on to it, you can feel where the tunnel gets lower, and you won't bang your head.'

'So, 'ow come you know so much?' Bos growled.

'I don't,' Leo said. 'I'm just trying to work it out as I go along. I can't see anything, so I can only go by touch. I'm not making out I'm clever, I'm just trying to get us out of here.'

They edged and stumbled their way along, for what seemed to Leo like an age. He could hear Bos's breathing behind him, and could smell him, too. He'd often wondered why Bos smelled so rank, like bad stew, or stale biscuits. He was so close that it began to make him want to throw up. At least, though, he told himself, it wasn't the smell of a Stealer, so, whatever else Bos was up to, he wasn't a Stealer in a shifted shape.

The thought made him feel at once safer, and yet more panicked. The Stealers could be anywhere, dressed as anything, and if he and Bos managed to get out, it would certainly not be the end of their troubles. He began to feel weary. The dark, the bone-chilling damp, and the seemingly interminable length of the passage made him wonder whether he had misinterpreted the Grolchen's message. At the point when his muscles were failing, and his eyes ached so much he wanted to close them and sleep, he glimpsed something up ahead.

'Light!' he shouted excitedly.

The cry reverberated around them ' ...*light! ...light!*' as the dripping walls absorbed the words and bounced them back to him.

Leo no longer feared the echoing, or the dungeon. He could see a small circle of light ahead, and he felt sure that it was a way out. The tunnel dipped suddenly, and they found themselves crouching down, forced to move forward on hands and knees. Leo crawled gingerly, feeling the hard ground through his jeans, knowing his knees would be bruised by the time he got out, but trying to concentrate on simply going forward. Water was dripping everywhere and, behind him, Bos was whining.

'This is 'opeless; we'll end up in the river, I bet. All this water,' he grumbled. 'Your fault if I drown.'

The light ahead became brighter and began to look like sky; a high, blue, jagged circle, with wisps of white cloud drifting across. Almost immediately, the tunnel swung upward into what looked like a steep, narrow chimney. Uneven, jutting stones offered foot-holds, and Leo eyed them warily, uncertain how safe they would be. However, the sight of the bright sky and the thought of getting out filled him with determination and renewed energy, and so, setting aside his doubts, he began to climb. It wasn't easy. He almost slipped more than once, and at some point, he dislodged a stone, which hurtled down, narrowly missing Bos, who was behind him.

'Mind what you're doin', you clumsy ass,' Bos shouted. 'That coulda' killed me!'

Leo almost wished it had, but he mumbled an apology. As he struggled on, he could hear Bos breathing heavily and swearing behind him. He had no idea how he was going to deal with him once they were out. He wanted him to disappear altogether, but he had a horrible feeling that wasn't going to happen. Suddenly, Leo was scrambling out of the tight hole, into fresh, delicious, open air.

'I'm out!' Leo cried, throwing his arms high.

He was on the hillside, well below the castle, standing in the midst of a large patch of bramble and nettles. Below him, not far away, the river tumbled and hissed over the rocks on its journey to the sea. Above his head, birds wheeled across the wide blue sky. Never had the open air seemed as wonderful as it did at that moment. Leo gazed around him and gratefully breathed his lungs full.

He began pushing his way out of the thicket, and turning, he saw Bos following. Bos was still scowling, still looking as though it was all someone else's fault. He didn't look around with pleasure, or express delight at being free, but pushed his way out of the hole, grimacing and griping. Leo took one last look at him and decided that his job, as far as Bos was concerned, was over. He'd got himself and Bos out, and wanted no more to do with him.

The sooner he was out of his presence the better, or he would lose his temper and say something to cause a fight. Besides which, he knew that where Bos was, the Stealer might be. It could still be a trap, and he wanted distance between them. He began to walk away, but Bos followed.

'Where are you going?' Leo asked, turning to face him.

'I'm follerin' you,' Bos said, sticking out his chin. 'Or 'ow will I get 'ome?'

'No you're not following me,' Leo said angrily. 'I'm heading back over that way.' He pointed to a path, which led up around the humped mound to a point where it entered the lower castle wall. 'You want to go that way.'

He pointed toward a downward path, which led away from the castle mound, and, he hoped, toward the town. Whoever had brought Bos here could take him away again. Leo was sick of the sight of him. Leo walked on, but he could hear Bos still scuffling along behind him.

'Look,' Leo shouted, 'you can't come with me. I'm with some friends. They don't want you along. Get it? Just bog off!'

He might as well have been talking to himself. Bos stopped briefly, but as soon as Leo began to walk, he followed again. Leo knew he could not keep up the pretence of not noticing this, and, finally, he stopped, heaved a huge sigh, and sat down on the grass beside the path. Bos sat down next to him.

'I won't let you come with me any further till you tell me what's going on and how you came to be in that dungeon.' Leo said.

'Can't stop me.' Bos cried. 'I'll just foller yer.'

Leo didn't move.

Bos scowled. 'I don't know what's goin' on meself,' he grunted. 'I did what 'e said, and look what 'appened. 'E threw me in that dungeon. Why did 'e do that?'

'How did you get here in the first place?' Leo asked.

Bos screwed up his face, as though he had to solve a deep and puzzling riddle. 'Gave me my fare and I got the bus,' he said, 'but I thought he'd give me some money to get back, once I got 'ere. 'E asked me to come. I din't want to go pokin' round an old castle.'

Leo was racking his brains, trying to think why the Stealer would send Bos to Cilgerran, if not to trap him and Ginny. If that was the reason, why had the Stealer not come down into the dungeon, captured Leo and let Bos go? It didn't make any sense. Unless the reason for Bos being there was something quite different, nothing to do with him and Ginny, and it had just been an unhappy accident that they'd found in the dungeon. Bos must know more than he was saying. Or, perhaps he didn't even *know* what he knew. He was so dull, so stupid; it was hard to imagine that he might be able to think something out and then actually keep secrets.

'Okay,' Leo said, 'I'll do a deal with you. I'm going to ask you some questions. You're going to tell me the truth. If you do, I'll give you your bus fare home. If I think you're lying, you walk.'

Bos started to shout, 'I'll foller...'

Leo cut him off. 'No, you won't,' he said, 'and, anyway, we've not come from Narberth. We're staying...' he paused, aware that he had almost given away where Izzy's house was, '...somewhere else,' he finished.

Seeing the defiant look on Bos's face, and using a sudden inspired memory of what Bos had seen in the dungeon, he continued,

'My animal friend, the one that got us out of the dungeon, remember? He'll do anything I ask him. I'll call him up and get him to chuck you over the edge. So, just shut up about following me.'

It did the trick. Bos shot a shifty look over his shoulder, and hunched further into his grimy sweatshirt.

'What do you do for this man that gives you money?' Leo asked.

Bos squirmed, but he seemed, in a way, to be relieved to be telling someone.

'When it started, the first time I met 'im, 'e said 'e'd give me a quid for the name of each one in my class, and where they lived. Easy – thirty quid, in two days.'

Leo caught his breath. Thanks to Bos and his greed for money, the Stealer now knew where he lived. He was so disgusted with Bos, it was an effort to stop himself getting up and walking away.

'Then?' he asked, gritting his teeth. 'What next?'

'Then, 'e said 'e'd see me at carnival. 'E gave me money to 'ang round near you lot.'

'What for?' Bos shrugged. 'What else did he want you to do?' Leo repeated.

'I din't want to do it. So I pushed your mate off that bin, instead,' Bos went silent, owlish. Head sank into his neck, he looked as though he had just remembered something that frightened him.

Leo's skin crawled. 'He wanted you to lead me to him, didn't he?' he said.

Bos's nod was small, but Leo saw it.

'So, tell me, why didn't you?' he asked.

Bos's voice took on a self-pitying, whining tone. 'I've 'eard of men doin' 'orrible things to kids, an' I jus' couldn't do it. 'E never did nowt to me. 'E wanted me to get you to chase me, get you away from the crowds. I could've, easy, but I kept thinkin', what did 'e want you for? 'E was mad when I din't get yer. 'E said 'e couldn't trust me, I was flabby like the rest of 'em. 'E said 'e wan't payin' me for startin' a fight, and stormed off. I thought that was it. Then, this mornin', 'e turns up again, right outside my 'ouse, and says 'e wants me to come 'ere, and 'e'd pay me what 'e owed me, and more, just to come 'ere an' look at a stinkin' old castle. I din't even know you'd be 'ere – I couldn't believe me eyes when you an' that girl turned up.'

'But you knew he'd be here?' Leo asked.

'Said 'e'd be waitin', with me money. Ha! Big joke. 'E puts 'is arm round my shoulder, all friendly, then pushes me down a flight of stone steps, and shuts me in. Look at my bruises.'

Leo had already seen them. Bos's face was swollen and bluish, all down one side, and his hands were badly grazed. He looked away, trying desperately to understand what had happened. He didn't yet know how the Stealer had sealed off the dungeon, but he was aware that, with the magic he had at his disposal, it was probably a relatively simple challenge. He'd thrown Bos down there because he was no longer to be trusted and, at the same time, conveniently, he could be used as bait to trap Leo. What is more, it had worked.

Had the Stealer simply meant to leave them there? The answer to that was probably yes. Who would ever think of looking behind a stone wall that looked as though it had been there for centuries?

If the Grolchen had not appeared, the plan may well have

worked. Leo knew that he himself would eventually have explored every possible route to an exit, but maybe the Stealer would have arrived before then, to work his will on Leo. He glanced at Bos, wondering how far the Stealer had affected him. Was he dead inside, like Gido said you would be if the Stealer got hold of your dreams? Maybe he was, but he couldn't be thoroughly bad, because he'd refused to turn Leo over to the Stealer, and that was surely an indication that he wasn't totally in the Stealer's power. That was, of course, if Bos had been telling the truth.

Obviously, the Stealer knew nothing of the passage in the hillside but, somehow, he had known that Leo and Ginny were coming that day. How?

As they walked back up towards the castle, Leo became aware of the presence of birds above them.

'Crows, aren't they?' he asked Bos, pointing toward them.

Bos squinted upwards. 'Yeah,' he said. 'Thousands of 'em.'

'I wonder what's wrong with them,' Leo said. 'They look sort of upset.'

He watched as they turned in the sky, and flew back in a straggling mass toward the castle ramparts, as though they'd been having a meeting and were heading home. Leo sighed and wondered if he was going mad, talking about birds being upset. They'd just been flying around normally, like birds did, and he, Leo, had just escaped from a filthy hole underground, and was more than grateful for the outdoors. He decided that the crows were harmless, ordinary birds. He squared his shoulders and continued the long uphill trudge. He'd try to be prepared to meet it, whatever lay ahead of him.

Chapter 7

HEAVY WEATHER

LEO STUMPED ALONG the beach, alone; he was dressed in anorak and Wellington boots, and he had his hood up and his head down against a chilly wind. Overnight, the weather had turned bad suddenly, and a fitful drizzle accompanied the wind, shrouding everything in a murky grey mist. The miserable day mirrored Leo's feelings.

He didn't want to be indoors, even though Izzy had lit a big fire in the living room, and pulled out jigsaws and games from cupboards and drawers, showing delight with every find, as though to tempt Leo and Ginny to remain indoors.

'Look, Scrabble! Oh, and here we have Millionaire, and Trivial Pursuit, and there's a great jigsaw here, that shows all the counties with their old names.'

On and on she went, but Leo was barely listening. He knew she was trying hard to get him and Ginny to talk to each other and enjoy themselves, but her kindly meant efforts were useless. Ginny was sulking. Leo knew why, but when Izzy asked him what was wrong, he simply shrugged.

'She's in a mood,' he said with finality. 'I'm going out for a walk.'

'In this weather?' Izzy queried, her eyebrows high, and her voice even higher. 'You're mad. Stay indoors and make up.'

Leo thought that sometimes Ginny behaved like a stupid kid,

and he didn't care if he seemed like an idiot to Izzy, when he insisted that he was going out. He had done nothing to Ginny for which he needed to apologise.

The sea wall, built by generations long gone, attracted his attention. He had never seen anything quite like it. It was a combination of horizontal and vertical slates, built close together, and held in place at intervals by huge slabs. He wished he could just enjoy looking at it, and, maybe, find out about it, instead of worrying about stuff that he couldn't understand. What he had said, to annoy Ginny, was that she should not have listened to the voice she *thought* she'd heard, that had told her to throw the dying crow over the walkway.

'That was cruel,' he said. 'Gido would never have told you to do that.'

Ginny had been furious that he hadn't believed her, and that he'd continued to argue for the poor bird.

'Poor bird?' she'd screamed at him. 'It was *one of them!*'

'I think it was one of them that told you to do it,' Leo said, 'and that's why you got attacked.'

'What?' Ginny was beside herself. 'You think it was all *my* fault?'

This argument had taken place late the previous evening, when they were both exhausted at the end of their mystifying day with the Halletts at Cilgerran. They were sitting outside on the little patio at the back of Izzy's house, trying to make some sense out of the days events.

'You!' spluttered Ginny in her outrage. 'You *think* you saw the Grolchen, and I believed you. So why don't you believe I saw Gido?' Before Leo could think of an answer, she had gabbled on.

'And, after everything that happened, you made Mr Hallett drive all the way to Narberth, specially to take that smelly, horrible boy home, and you kept us waiting outside for ages, while you went into his poxy little house. Mrs Hallett said you were the *rudest* boy she'd ever met in her *life*. And I think you probably are!'

She'd stormed off then, and slammed her bedroom door so hard it, seemed to make the whole house shake.

That the Halletts were fed up with him, too, came as no surprise. He stood still, as the wind lashed him and the drizzle thickened to drenching rain. He found himself staring at the slates in the wall, seeing nothing, only remembering what had happened and trying to make sense of it.

He had been unable to shake off Bos, when they had reached the castle, even though he had given him his bus fare home. When Leo looked around for Ginny and the Halletts, he'd had a nasty shock. It was their shrieks and screams that told him where they were, and he ran as fast as his bruised legs would take him, in the direction of the sounds. At the archway leading into the grassy inner ward, he and Bos were horrified at the sight that met his eyes.

The air was filled with flapping wings and loud, raucous cawing. Hundreds of birds were circling and swooping down on Mr and Mrs Hallett and the three girls. They ran around in confusion and panic, covering their heads with their arms and shrieking, as the mass of winged attackers spiralled down on them, again and again, their beaks open, their wings beating the air like a vast airborne army.

'This way, this way,' shouted Mr Hallett, waving his arms in all directions, whilst trying to get the others to follow him to the archway. 'Stay calm. They'll go away. Don't let them see you're frightened.'

One by one, they stumbled through the opening and onto the outer grass, where Leo stood gaping. Bos was leaning over his shoulder trying to see what was going on.

'It's them birds we saw,' he said, and for a moment Leo thought he sounded pleased, amused.

As the Halletts rushed past him, Leo saw the birds flock together and fly upward, high up above the height of the towers. Then, circling rapidly, they zoomed suddenly downward toward the bewildered group. The noise of their wings and cawing was deafening.

'Run!' Mr Hallett yelled at the top of his voice, and ran off toward the outer gate.

Everyone followed him, including Leo and Bos, down the path and out onto the lane. The birds did not follow this time. They stayed within the confines of the castle, flocking and breaking, soaring and rolling.

'What was all that about?' panted Leo, leaning against a wall, catching his breath.

'*She* threw a crow over the bridge,' shrieked Mrs Hallett, pointing at Ginny. 'That's what. They all came after us, and it was *her* fault.'

Mr Hallett looked back to where the birds still wheeled and turned in the sky.

'Rooks,' he announced, as he wiped his sweating forehead with his sleeve. 'Not crows; rooks. I should've known. Why didn't I look at that one properly? They wouldn't have attacked us if we'd helped that one that was injured. I wish I'd done it now.

They live in families, like human beings, and we've upset them.'

Everyone looked at Ginny, who stared straight ahead, saying nothing. Her cheeks were red and there was a frown on her brow.

'Where on earth did you get to?' Mr Hallett asked Leo, as though he'd only just noticed he was there.

'I was exploring,' Leo claimed uncertainly. 'Got a bit lost.'

Mrs Hallett and the girls were staring at Bos in undisguised disgust.

'You shouldn't have wandered off on your own,' Mrs Hallett snapped, 'and who's that?' She pointed at Bos.

Bos began to cry, or pretended to, and through his crocodile tears, he begged for a lift home, saying he was a friend of Leo's who had, like him, got lost, and been left behind by friends. Leo was angry when he heard this. Narberth was miles out of their way. He could, he knew, have said indignantly, 'He's no friend of mine and I've already given him his fare home,' but he was dumbstruck by Bos's nerve, and unable to stop Bos's clever manipulation of the Halletts without making himself look mean and nasty.

Mr Hallett could not refuse Bos's tearful pleas, though he was hardly happy about it, and no one else looked very cheerful either. The trip to Narberth was long and uncomfortable. The Bos smell factor made everyone feel ill, and Leo could have died of embarrassment at the thought that the Halletts believed he was a close friend of his.

Then, when they arrived at Bos's house, in a broken down, semi-derelict terrace, Mr Hallett had insisted that Leo go in with Bos, to explain to his parents what had happened. Leo thought Mr Hallett was probably expecting someone to come out and thank him. Leo saw inside the house, and as his shocked eyes took in the scene, he knew there was no way that the drunken figure on the battered sofa, surrounded by cans and bottles, would get up to thank anyone.

Bos's house was filthy. There was hardly a stick of furniture in it, and it was dark and cold. It made Leo feel sick and it confused him, too. Something inside him told him he should feel sorry for Bos, and a part of him did, but, also, he couldn't wait to get away.

'Give me the fare back, Bos,' he'd said.

Bos had shaken his head.

'Yer give it me, din't yer?' he jeered. 'Yer din't lend it me, yer give it me.'

Leo had tried to insist but Bos had stood his ground. 'I in't givin' it yer, so just bog off,' he'd said.

The gross figure on the sofa had opened a bleary eye. 'You got money?' it had croaked at Bos.

'No.'

The figure had moved forward, grabbing Bos viciously by the arm as he tried to pass. 'Don't you lie to me, you little ghoul. I 'eard what you said. Give it 'ere.' Then the man had looked at Leo, and Leo had decided it was not worth waiting for an introduction to Bos's parent, on a matter of two pounds. He had fled, slamming the door behind him and climbing back into the safety of the Halletts' smart people-carrier, without uttering a word.

Mr Hallett had been in a dreadful state and not driving well. On top of the fact that his good-natured wife had been seated beside him, nagging him about all his faults as though they'd been building up inside her for the past fifteen years, he'd had no luck with his wonderful metal detector, which was now certainly broken, after being blown around the tower. Being chased by the birds had been the last straw, on an already awful day. The girls were silent and sulky throughout the jerky ride. Now and again, when Mr Hallett had taken a corner too suddenly and they were all thrown into each other, one of them would bleat, 'Da...ad!'

During the drive, Leo and Ginny had been unable to speak about what had happened. They knew they would have to talk later, but not in front of the Halletts, and they had sat in silence, and longed to be home.

Leo turned his back to the wind, and leaned against the sea wall. He wanted to think carefully and be clear in his head about what had happened. He genuinely thought Ginny had been mistaken in thinking that Gido had given her the instruction to kill the injured crow. If it was the right thing to do, why had the birds chased them?

One of the Stealers must have spoken to her, intent on turning the birds against the Halletts. Leo could think of no reason for this. The birds had not actually harmed anyone, just whizzed around.

His mind went back to the scene, and conjured up the image of birds diving and rising, skimming around the terrified group and, for a moment, he was taken with the strange idea that they appeared not only to be trying to scare the Hallett family, but to be *looking* for something.

Suddenly, other things popped into his head. There had been the crows flying above the sea, attacking the seagull. He remembered the birds hovering above him and Bos, when they stumbled out of the passage from the dungeon. A weird thought occurred to him. Could any of these birds by the sea have been there spying for the Stealers?

The man in the shop had told Mrs Hallett that people didn't seem to want to come to the castle, and he had spoken of the strange mist that he'd never seen before. *'And the birds...'* he'd said.

Leo thought of the Grolchen, appearing and disappearing in the tunnel, and he began to feel ashamed. He had not doubted his own sighting of one of the Keepers, though it had been brief, and it had proved to be right because he'd followed directions and got out of the dungeon. He decided that he had been totally unfair in dismissing Ginny's story of meeting Gido as pure imagination. Just because he, Leo, didn't know what was going on, there was no reason to think that Ginny couldn't tell the difference between a Stealer and Gido.

Reluctantly, he realised that, indeed, he should go back and apologise to Ginny. He'd cut her off in the middle of her story, which was not just unkind, it was stupid. She may have picked up clues that were important, and because he'd been so stubborn, he hadn't waited to find out what they might have been. He turned and began to walk slowly back to the house, muttering to himself and kicking at loose stones.

'We need to talk to the Keepers. They'd know what it was all about, and could advise us what we should do next. I wish I knew what 'The Way' was that Gido said would lead us to them. I'm sure it was carrig something. I should've listened.'

At the front door of Izzy's, he took a deep breath. Apologising was not an easy thing to do, and he still wasn't sure that he'd been in the wrong. However, he had to give Ginny a chance to finish her report. Ginny was lying on the living room floor, doing a jigsaw. She looked up at him, then, looked away. Her face was unfriendly.

'Sorry,' Leo said. She didn't raise her eyes from the jigsaw. 'I think I was a bit er...' A long pause followed before she looked up at him, her eyes narrowed.

'What?' she snapped. 'A bit what? A bit wrong? A bit mean? A bit arrogant, maybe?'

'All of those,' he sighed, flopping into a nearby easy chair. 'Listen, Ginny, I'm confused. I heard what Mrs Hallett said, and then what Mr Hallett said about them being rooks, and I thought they must be right.'

Izzy had come in as he was speaking and heard what he was saying. 'What's this about rooks?' she asked pleasantly. 'Were you bird-spotting yesterday?'

They looked at each other, wondering what to tell her. If she bumped into the Halletts, when the weather improved, they would no doubt give her a blow-by-blow account of what had happened at the castle, as seen from their point of view.

'Some birds chased us,' Ginny said casually, looking back at the jigsaw. 'We're trying to figure out why.'

'Tell me more,' Izzy said.

'There was a big black bird, Aunty Izzy, and it fell on the walkway between the towers,' Ginny said, not looking up. 'It was dying, and I threw it over the top of the rail, so that it would fall onto the rocks and have a quick death.'

'That was a very strange thing for you to have done,' Izzy said, looking surprised. 'But, if you were sure it couldn't be helped, and you were high enough for it to die outright when it landed, I suppose it seems like the kindest thing to have done.'

Ginny perked up. 'D'you really think so?' she asked. 'I'm glad, because the others didn't think so, and the other birds didn't either. They chased us around, cawing and flapping.'

'Goodness!' Izzy's eyes were large. 'A lot of them, were there, or only a few?'

'Hundreds,' Leo said.

'And you think they were rooks?'

Leo nodded.

Izzy looked thoughtful for a minute. 'And the Halletts? What did they think?'

'They thought the rooks chased us because of what I'd done,' Ginny said.

'Maybe,' Izzy said thoughtfully, 'if they were rooks, it can be explained. I think I read somewhere that, if a member of a rook parliament dies, the other birds do become agitated. On the other hand, Ginny, they may have been expressing their gratitude. They didn't actually attack you, did they?'

'No, just flapped and cawed and came really close.' Ginny said.

'Parliament?' Leo repeated, staring at Izzy.

'That's what a family group of rooks is called,' Izzy said. 'I have an interesting book about birds. I must look it out for you to read.'

Leo could hardly hide the look that came to his face.

'*They've pulled in the parliament…*' Gido had said.

Ginny had been right, after all. She had done the only possible thing that had to be done, when she threw the bird over the edge. The Stealers were amongst them, inside the parliament, or controlling the birds.

He felt a surge of excitement at the thought of Ginny having outwitted them, whilst he was below ground making his escape.

'You did good,' he said to Ginny, with a broad grin, to show he wanted to be friends.

'I know,' Ginny said, and though she didn't return his smile, he could tell she wasn't still angry with him.

'Lunch is ready,' Izzy said, 'and the rain seems to be slowing down. Maybe, you'll be able to get some fresh air this afternoon.'

She did not refer to their morning dispute at all, and Leo was grateful that she had proved to be a useful source of information, and she minded her own business, too. It suddenly crossed his mind that there may be other things she might know, and he put it to the test by asking,

'Have you ever heard of 'The Way' – 'Carrig' something-or-other?' He followed her to the big kitchen, where steaming pots of spicy beans and rice sat on the big pine table.

'Carreg Coetan Arthur.' Izzy said without hesitation.

'You've heard of it?' Leo could hardly keep the thrill from his voice.

'Yes, it's just down the road,' Izzy said. 'It's a Neolithic stone burial chamber. In ancient times, the people took it to be one of the entrances to the Otherworld, Annwn. That's why it's called The Way. People don't believe things like that any more, so the name's lost to most. Who told you it was called that?

'My teacher, I think,' Leo crossed his fingers, 'but he didn't mention Arthur. It might not be the right place.'

How had Gido known he could find it so easily? It was almost as though the Keepers had known where he would be.

'King Arthur wasn't Neolithic,' smiled Izzy, as she ladled out their meal. 'Later generations added his name to the most significant ancient sites all over Britain. Anywhere that people considered special before he came along had Arthur's name attached to them. Thus, Coetan Arthur is supposed to be where he played quoits. The word quoit actually means a circle, or an open ring, and its ancient meaning was an entrance.' She put her hands together to form a circle. 'Like so.' She beamed at them. 'I'm glad you're interested in history. I'll dig out a book on Neolithic sites for you and you can study it if the weather gets worse. On the other hand, you could walk over there after lunch, if it brightens up a bit.'

The rain had virtually disappeared by the time Leo and Ginny stepped outdoors to make their way to Carreg Coetan. This was their chance to talk privately, and they brought each other up to date with what had happened to them at the castle. Leo listened intently to Ginny's description of the metal detector incident, and asked to see the tin lid she had found. Ginny delved in her pocket for it. The second Leo touched it he knew what it was. His heart beat faster, and he felt the hairs on the back of his neck prickle. This was Manawl's brooch!

The knowledge stunned him. It looked like a valueless bit of tin; yet in his hand, it felt like gold; soft, glossy, and weighty. He rolled it in his palm, opened his hand and looked at it again. For a split second, he saw an intricate, beautiful piece of jewellery, and when he blinked in astonishment, it turned back into an old tin lid. This was why the rooks had been following them, and why he and Ginny had been sent to Cilgerran. This was what Gido had wanted them to find.

'It's funny,' Ginny was saying, 'Mr Hallett, or Jimbo, as he said I can call him, said it was worthless. When I held it in my hand, it felt too heavy, and looked too shiny to be worthless. I thought it might polish up or something.'

Leo, fondling the object, felt it could be any shape, any colour, any precious metal it chose to be. It was an extraordinary thing, a solid, but totally fluid, piece of something, which changed as he moved it.

'Now that is clever,' he breathed. 'That is very clever.'

'What is?'

'It's alive,' Leo said. 'Take it.' He passed it to her. 'Just move it about in your hand.'

Ginny flexed her fingers and allowed the lid to roll down her hand.

'Oh!' she gasped. 'It feels like pieces of glass, or are they diamonds, or pearls, or something?'

'You know what it is?' Leo said excitedly. He had an odd feeling that shouldn't say Manawl's name out loud, though he had no idea who might be able to hear it. He and Ginny were alone. They had just entered a lane that bore a signpost for Carreg Coetan. There were neat bungalows with colourful gardens on either side of where they stood, but apart from cars standing on the tidy driveways, there was no sign of life anywhere. He looked back up the lane, to where they had turned off, and looked back down the length of lane beyond them. He could see for a good distance, and there was no one else around.

He looked up instinctively, to see whether there were any large black birds nearby. In a bank of trees, some two hundred yards away, he saw two birds flying between the branches, but they didn't look as though they were interested in Leo and Ginny. They might be, though, he thought.

'It's the brooch,' he said softly. 'That's why the rooks were chasing you. I *knew* they were looking for something. We've got the brooch. And we may have rescued the castle too, because this is what they were there for, and they won't hang around now we have it.'

'No,' Ginny sniffed, walking on, 'but I don't know why you're looking so happy. It just means the Stealers will come after us instead.'

Chapter 8

WAY-FINDER

THEY TOOK a turn off the lane, where a narrow path snaked between the bungalows.

'Are you sure we're going in the right direction?' Ginny asked in a hushed voice. 'I feel like we're walking in someone's garden.'

'Maybe we are,' Leo said, 'but the sign pointed this way, and I can't see any other path. Nobody's stopping us anyway.'

They arrived at a small wooden gate, set in a hedge. Beyond it stood the burial chamber, a hump-backed stone pile, in a grassy plot the size of a small paddock, enclosed by fences, bushes and trees. Leo was shocked. Somehow, he had imagined it out in the open, on a windswept hillside, like the stones at Gors Fawr. They stood at the gate, uncertain about entering.

'It is public, isn't it?' Ginny asked. 'It looks kind of private.'

She glanced down at the brooch, still clutched in her hand. It had begun to feel hot, and though it really did look like a bent old tin lid, it had begun to feel heavy, as if it was made of lead. It made her feel uncomfortable, as though she was carrying a weight too great for her body. It was as if it had sat happily in her pocket whilst she believed it to be a tin lid, but now it wanted her to let it go. She was afraid she might drop it, or lose it, if she held on to it.

'What did Gido want us to do with the brooch if we found it?' she asked.

'Give it to him, I suppose,' Leo said. 'I think it's dangerous if it gets into the Stealer's hands, and I'm not surprised. I never felt anything like it. I bet, if you knew how to use it, you could do powerful things.'

'You mean, if you knew the right words and things?' Ginny asked, still looking at it.

Leo had no idea how it might work, he simply knew it was capable of something amazing. He would have liked to keep it long enough to discover its secret, but he knew he could not do that.

Ginny held it out to him and said, 'Gido came to you. It was an accident that I found it. You were meant to find it, and you're meant to have it.'

Leo longed to take it, but he was afraid he would never want to let go of it again.

'You found it,' he said. 'Put it back in your pocket.'

'I wasn't looking for it,' Ginny insisted. 'It was just a trick, to get Mr Hallett to come with me while I looked for you, when I suggested going down into the bottom of the tower and using his metal-detector. I don't want to keep this.' A stubborn look came to her face that Leo knew well.

'Why can't you hang onto it for now? We're going to give it Gido, anyway, when we meet him next.'

Ginny struggled to explain that she was afraid of the power of this thing moving in her hand, without sounding weak and girlie.

'Manawl was a man, right?' she asked.

'Of course he was,' said Leo. 'He was the greatest magician and shapeshifter ever, and he was around long before Merlin or any other wizard.'

Ginny said, 'Some things are meant for men and some are meant for women. This is a man's thing. Go on, Leo, you take it.'

'Okay,' Leo said, 'if you're sure. But if you change your mind...'

'I won't,' she answered.

Leo took it, felt its weight and heat, and slid it into a small secret pocket on the inside of his anorak. It rested against his heart, he felt it flutter there like a small bird, and then it was still, and light as a tin lid. It made his skin flush and tingle. He opened the little gate leading to the burial chamber, a cluster of upright stones with a huge lichen-covered slab laid across their tops. A sudden flash of sunshine lighted the golden colour of the lichen briefly. For a second, Leo was dazzled. He held his breath. He'd harboured a sneaking doubt that Izzy's Arthur stones were not The Way. Now, he began to believe it, and, as if to confirm his thoughts, he felt a twitch from the object in his inside pocket. This was the place.

'Carreg Coetan,' he said. 'The Way.'

Ginny gazed at the burial chamber. 'Neolithic,' she said. 'How long ago was that?'

'Thousands of years,' Leo responded.

'You mean, it's stood here for all that time?'

'*Much* longer than most buildings last,' Leo said.

'I wonder how many dead people were buried here,' Ginny said, her voice sounding uncertain.

Leo was walking around it, trying to figure out how anyone could describe anything about this place as a circle, or an entrance. It looked to have neither circle nor entrance. There were spaces between the stones, and a sandy floor in the centre. One side of the enormous capstone was covered with the glowing lichen, which, up close, appeared to be copper coloured. Leo touched it. It tickled his fingers.

Below his feet, deep in the ground, he felt a throbbing sensation. It was so brief he wondered whether he'd imagined it. The tin lid in his pocket twitched again, as if it too had felt it.

What was he supposed to do next? He started by examining every visible surface of the stones. On one side, a deep narrow cleft between two upright stones had the appearance of a structured crack, a chiselled chink to somewhere else. He put his eye to the gap and looked through it. He could see the leaves of a holly tree, on the opposite side of the plot, and beyond it, the view extended out across the estuary.

He felt disappointment mixed with relief. There was no 'entrance' to anywhere, and, even if there had been, he wondered whether he would he have gone into it. After his experience in the dungeon, he doubted if he would have happily climbed down into a hole in the ground.

Ginny had wandered off across the paddock, tracing an ever widening downward spiral, moving away from the stones themselves and following the shape of the mound that signified the burial ground. At its edge, where hedges and trees blocked her further progress, she paused.

'I think, if this whole hill was a burial ground, it would be huge, wouldn't it?' Ginny said, trying to imagine what it had been like when the long-ago people had built it.

'Not necessarily, Leo said. 'It depends whether it was meant for one person, or for a whole tribe, I suppose.'

'What are we supposed to do, anyway, now we've got here?' she asked.

'I'm not sure,' Leo said. 'In fact, I've no idea.'

'I think we should just sit by it,' Ginny said. 'Do you remember the stone at Gors Fawr, when we sat beside it and heard those voices?'

'That was because the Keepers were trapped inside the stone,' Leo said. 'There'd be no point to us doing it here.'

'Can you think of something better?' Ginny asked.

Leo shook his head. Ginny sat down with her back to the stones, facing the holly tree and the distant glimpse of the estuary. The grass was damp, but she hitched her anorak down and sat on it.

'I think it's about words,' Ginny said. 'You know when we went to them before, when we were at the observatory?'

He nodded. 'But it was the dogs that took us,' he said.

'I know,' Ginny said, 'Do you remember, when we were there, they gave us words. One of them was the key word that let us get back to our world, but the same word might work to get us into their world. You remember it, don't you?'

'Garloyg Molp,' Leo said.

He leaned again toward the stone and peeped through the crack. There were a man, a woman and a dog, standing under the holly tree. Leo jumped. No one had entered the plot through the gate, whilst he and Ginny had been there, and there was no other access into the enclosed space. He stepped away from the narrow crack, and looked straight across to where he'd seen them. They were still there, smiling and nodding. Ginny saw them too, and leapt to her feet, not sure whether they were real or if she was imagining them.

Leo said, 'Hello.'

The dog sang a greeting in a strange off-key warble, and turned to shake his rear in the children's direction.

'Grolchen!' Leo laughed, and moved toward them, but as he did this, they seemed to melt away, and quickly disappeared, as suddenly as they had arrived.

'They've gone!' Ginny cried.

'What happened?' Leo was stunned. 'It *was* them. Wasn't it?'

He ran across to the holly tree and looked around it. There was a narrow path, which seemed to extend from its roots and led into the plot, not out of it. There was no way out that he could see, through the deep hedge on either side.

'It's just the same as at the castle,' he groaned. 'They're having difficulty getting through, but they said this was a good place to meet them, so why did they disappear?'

A noise of flapping wings and cawing made both of them turn. To their alarm, they watched a number of large black birds zoom down and land on the high hedge behind them.

'That explains it,' muttered Leo. 'I hope they're not thinking of ambushing us, like they did before.'

Ginny looked nervously at the birds. She had hated being chased by them, and did not intend it to happen again. Amongst them could be the two Stealers, whose ability to change shape she didn't doubt, after the experience on the walkway.

'P'raps we should just leave,' she said, and began to move toward the gate.

Leo was still standing next to the burial chamber, watching the birds, his hand resting on the lichen-covered slab.

Ginny hesitated. 'Are you coming?' she called.

He shook his head and moved his free hand to his inside pocket.

For a wild moment, Ginny thought he was going to offer the brooch to the birds. But Leo was not trying to get it out of his pocket. He was holding it hidden in his jacket. With one hand still laid on the roof of the burial chamber, and the other hand on the brooch, very loudly and deliberately, he cried out, 'Plom gyolrag.'

If Leo had thought saying the magic words backwards would open the Way and allow him to travel into Gido's world, he was mistaken. However, something did happen. The sound of a dog's bark from near to the gate made Ginny start and turn, and caused the birds to take off in a sudden flurry of panic. A sleek, grey dog, with bright eyes and a tail as sharp and pointed as his nose, stood gazing up at her.

If the standing stones had opened and showed them a flight of steps to another dimension, Ginny could not have been more surprised.

She leapt toward the gate, threw it open, and hugged the animal enthusiastically.

'Basil,' she cried, 'what are you doing here?'

'He's a Wayfinder,' Leo said, his hand still on the brooch, and a puzzled look on his face. 'It's a funny thing, that I should know that. The brooch...' he stopped.

He had been going to say that the brooch had told him, but that was impossible. It had simply tingled, and knowledge of Basil's skill had popped into his head, accompanied by memories of the previous occasion when Basil had appeared and led him to meet Gido and friends.

'At the observatory,' he said. 'He took me there. He found the way then, if you remember.'

'But we're miles from home,' Ginny said. 'How could he do it on these little legs? Amazing!'

She was still stroking him and cooing affectionately, when Basil wriggled out of her hands and took off toward the burial chamber. He ran round it once, with his nose to the ground, then headed toward the holly tree, where he sniffed about. Then, looking back at them briefly, he turned and began to burrow his way through the thick hedge, and, as suddenly as he had appeared, he disappeared through the foliage. They heard him yelping from the other side of the hedge.

'Stupid animal!' shouted Leo. 'Come back!'

Basil stayed where he was, yelping and barking.

'He wants us to follow him,' Ginny said.

'Follow him?' cried Leo. 'We can't. How can we get through there? Look, there's a fence running through the hedge, and there's barbed wire all over it, and there's no way through.'

'P'raps we should go on our bellies,' Ginny argued. 'He managed it, didn't he? If we lie down like him, and wriggle through, we should be able to do it.'

'But he's going the wrong way,' Leo said in exasperation. 'We want him in here, by the burial chamber; not out there. And, if we do get through, how do we get back?'

Even as he said it, he knew he was wrong. The brooch was twitching and jerking in his pocket, pulling him down toward the ground and towards the tiny gap beneath the thorny bushes. Basil clearly had more idea of where he was going, than either he or Ginny had.

'Okay,' he sighed.

He got down on the wet grass and began to work his way

forward between the tangle of tree trunks and brambles. Ginny was already down on hands and knees, looking for a space, and beginning to push through.

★ ★ ★

It seemed that they had hardly started to find their way through, when they were out on the other side. It was as if they'd only thought about it, and it had happened.

Leo felt that there should have been a degree of discomfort, perhaps a sting from a thorn, or a struggle between branches, but there wasn't. He had simply lain down, lifted a bunch of leaves and looked into the undergrowth, prepared to scramble through it. Then, he was there, standing upright, with not a scratch, a speck of mud or a damp patch on him. Ginny stood beside him, equally suddenly, and without difficulty. Basil sat at their feet, tail thumping the ground and eyes agleam with satisfaction.

'We're somewhere else,' Leo said, looking round.

'It's like going to a hot country!' Ginny exclaimed, pulling off her anorak.

Leo did the same. The sudden change in temperature and brightness was alarming. It could not be due to the sun spilling through the clouds of the dreary day they had left behind. This was something else altogether. Leo couldn't even see the sun, but he could feel its heat, and the brightness that accompanied it was dazzling.

He squinted down the meadow that stretched away to the estuary. The water shimmered silver, and seemed much nearer and wider than it had been before.

In his pocket, the brooch was growing so much heavier that he needed to reach in and remove it. It was weighing him down like a huge stone.

'Something's happening to the brooch,' he announced.

He drew it out carefully, but it had become so heavy that he couldn't hold it in one hand. As he clutched at it with his other hand, it fell to the ground.

He stooped to pick it up, but Ginny grabbed at his back.

Don't!' she cried. 'Look what's happening to it!'

It was growing. At first it grew to the size of a round plate, and took on a golden glow so bright they had to shield their eyes. Then the circular shape changed to rectangular. The gold melted apart and became fine lines, which ran in patterns like writing, and as they stared at what had been a small piece of jewellery, it became a large, brown, leather-bound book. On its cover, in old-fashioned gold letters, were the words *Defnydd Hud*. They stared.

'Look at that!' Ginny exclaimed.

'Welsh,' Leo said. 'It means Magic Material. It's a book of spells.'

They gazed at it, baffled by its sudden appearance.

'That's exactly what it is,' said a voice behind them, making them jump.

There stood Gido, smiling.

'It is the brooch in your world, but shows its true self here in Dreamworld. You may have guessed what it is capable of. Manawl, the greatest shapeshifter ever, made it. He wore it always, as a brooch, to fasten his cloak. Each time he discovered a new spell, a new wisdom, he put another tiny piece of silver or gold into it. It is a *grimoire* of the highest order. Or, put more simply, the biggest magical text book that anyone could ever find.'

Leo let out a whistle of astonishment. 'No wonder you wanted it!' he said.

'Me?' Gido asked, looking at him in surprise. 'I don't want it, Leo. What would I use it for?'

'You'm 'oo found it,' Maria said, approaching from behind Gido, with the Grolchen at her heels.

'But you asked me to get it for you!' Leo said. 'And, anyway, it was Ginny who found it.'

'She did,' Gido agreed, 'and without Ginny, you would have been unable to fulfil the task.' He turned and smiled at her. 'The Stealer on the walkway was most effectively dealt with.'

'It *was* you.' Ginny said.

'It was,' Gido said. 'It was a dangerous moment. If you had not thrown that bird when you did, he could have brought in an attack on the walkway. That would have been a far more uncomfortable experience than on the ground, I warn you. Above ground, you are in their element: air. There is no doubt that all of you on the walkway could have been wiped out.'

Leo and Ginny gaped at him.

'True, every wordin' of it,' said Maria. 'And it wan't easy. No one like going through a worm-'ole on the outer circle. Even Grolchen were left with a greamy 'ead, rescuin' Leo.'

The Grolchen was eyeing Basil with a look of pure anticipation. His lively pink face was lit with the prospect of a chase, or a game. Basil, however, suddenly and unexpectedly, had fallen into a deep sleep. Ginny thought this was curious, in view of what was going on around him. She bent toward him, to see if he was all right.

'He's fine,' Gido said, seeing her concern. 'He came a long

way to find you. Let him rest now, before he takes you back home to your own dimension.'

Leo was still looking at the book. It seemed to be inviting him to open its pages but he resisted, still not sure that it was for him to touch it. Gido was watching him.

'You know we were the ones who sent you to Cilgerran. The postcard was the key, of course, and you did well. It was a most effective homing device.'

Leo looked incredulous.

'How do you know about the postcard?' Ginny asked.

'We could hardly leave it to chance that you and Leo would actually find your way to the Castle,' Gido said. 'We simply took some of its power of place, wrapped it in cardboard, and dropped it into Leo's pocket at the bus stop.'

'Weird,' Ginny said.

Leo found his voice. 'The postcard led me to Cilgerran?' he asked. 'I don't think so. It was Mr Hallett. I mean, I didn't want to go.'

'Precisely,' Gido agreed, 'but you did go. Sometimes, Leo, the happiest coincidences are no such thing. They are a part of the magnetic force that operates between human beings and places. One day, you will understand a great deal more of this magnetism. The brooch will teach you.'

'But it isn't a brooch any more,' Leo said. 'It's an enormous book.'

Gido just smiled. 'You will, of course, take on the task associated with Manawl. The brooch can assist you in sending the Dreamstealers to Neptune. Manawl foretold that, with his magical knowledge in the right hands, the Dreamstealers would eventually be stopped and dispatched to their brothers.'

'We hated doing it, last time,' Leo said quietly. He looked at Ginny, as though hoping for moral support before he continued. He saw from the set of her mouth and the determined look in her eye that she felt exactly as he did.

'Maybe they are zombies,' Leo began. 'I mean, we understand that they're half-alive and half-dead, and that they would be better with Neptune, but to us it still felt like killing someone. I hate the Dreamstealers as much as anyone would if they knew what they did, but watching his terror and everything was horrible.'

'I didn't really mind at the time,' Ginny said suddenly. 'I think I was just so glad to see the back of him, but I did afterwards. I thought about it a lot since, and I don't want to do it again.'

Gido, Maria and the Grolchen all nodded in turn. The Grolchen added a determined 'Mic.'

'I don't want to do it,' Ginny repeated, watching their faces wondering why they looked as though they agreed with everything she and Leo had said.

'We came to bring you the brooch and to say we think Cilgerran will be okay now,' said Leo carefully. 'We didn't think we still had to get the other two Stealers. We can't do it, Gido. It is not possible.'

'Think of it this way,' Gido said persuasively, 'if you don't go after them, they will still come after you. At some point, you must fight this battle, like it or not. When you helped us out of the stone, when you assisted us in sending their brother back to Neptune, when you stole Manawl's treasure from under their nose, when you escaped their time-shifting and shapeshifting tricks, you took it on. They have become more determined to catch you than you realise.'

'Oh good,' Leo said sarcastically. 'I happen to think that if we ignore them, and just…'

'You'm much mistook there,' Maria interrupted. 'Them can't be ignoored. You get openin' they pagelikes, and fin' out what to do.'

Leo felt cornered. He didn't want to be involved. He wanted to walk away, go home, and say goodbye to the whole lot of it, but he was also itching to have a look at what was inside the book.

'I don't know where to start,' he said. He looked at Ginny.

She shrugged. 'Don't ask me,' she said. 'I'm just glad I gave it to you, when I felt it was too heavy for me.'

'I'll tell you now where and how to start. Start by asking the question in your head,' Gido said. 'Then, think of a number and tell the number to Ginny.'

Leo tried to concentrate. He thought he would like to ask how the Stealers could be sent to Neptune, without him and Ginny feeling so bad about it. Then, a number popped into his head.

'A hundred and twenty nine,' he declared.

'Turn to that page, Ginny,' Gido said, pointing to the book.

Ginny got to her knees and turned the fine, golden-edged pages of the book.

'Right,' she said.

'Read for us,' Gido said.

Ginny began to read aloud, haltingly. The book was in a language that was like Welsh, but not quite the Welsh with which she was familiar. It seemed to have some other language woven into it. Ginny had no idea how to pronounce some of the words but she struggled through the twelve gold lines, clearly written in a strong hand, on the centre of the page.

'In English?' she asked Leo when she finished. 'Something about catching mists in a mirror and making pies in heaven, wasn't it?'

'Something like that,' Leo said shaking his head doubtfully.

'You'll find out,' Gido said. 'Between you, you've activated the spell. Once spoken, it cannot be undone.'

'But, Gido, it didn't mean anything,' Leo protested.

'All spells mean something,' Gido said. 'For instance, a mirror is one of a magician's tools. If you think the word is in the spell, then hold the book in your hand and command it to show you Manawl's mirror.'

Leo lifted the book. It was lighter than he expected, after the extraordinary weight it had gained while in his pocket, and he held it firmly in two hands, still open at page one hundred and twenty nine.

'Show me the mirror,' he declared, sounding a lot more certain than he felt. No sooner had he spoken than the words on the page began to change. The letters became small running figures, clustering together, holding hands to form an oval shape with an opening at the top. Silver water poured through the opening, filling the shape as though it was a vase. Once full, the flow quivered to a stop. Leo saw his own reflection, and Ginny's face beside his. Her curiosity had made her jump up to have a look at what was happening, and she stood at his shoulder and gasped.

'It *is* a mirror!' she exclaimed.

Then, it misted over and the silver surface disappeared beneath swirling coils of white vapour. When it cleared, their reflected images had gone and, in their place, a man had appeared. He wore a dark suit and had black crinkly hair, and a wide smile.

'The Dreamstealer,' Leo gasped, as the familiar figure from their adventure at the stone circle appeared. This time, those dreaded eyes were different, not burning as they had been, when they'd met before. He stood facing them and, with a flourish, he took a pack of cards from his pocket and fanned them. He walked toward them, offering the cards, as though he was about to do a trick. As he came nearer into the vaporous mirror, he melted away.

The mirror was quivering and returning to water, draining upwards, as though sucked up by an invisible force, the letters running back to where they had been on the page, like obedient little people taking up their familiar positions.

'Whoa! Did you see that?' Ginny cried. 'It was him! But he looked happy and normal.'

'What was it about?' Leo asked. 'What has a pack of cards got to do with anything?'

Gido threw back his head and laughed.

'It depends what your question was. What I can tell you, because I have followed his progress since that dreadful day, is that, in his sleep-time, between lives, he dreams of becoming a conjurer. The taste of magic he savoured will never leave him, but he is no longer a slave to his burnt and blackened soul. He hopes he will make a splendid, though tricky, entertainer in his next life.'

'I'm not sure what I think about that,' Leo frowned.

He thought of questions he would like to ask and looked at Gido and the others, wondering whether they were 'between lives', and what it meant. Words gathered in his mind, but he couldn't make them into sounds. He suddenly felt himself small and far away, like a wraith floating above everything. He wondered whether he had fallen asleep, everything seemed so distant and apart. The book fluttered in his hands, and began to move and shrink. Then, as though in a dream, he felt it creep like a mouse up his sleeve and into his inside pocket.

With a rush of wind and a thud, his back hit the stone of the burial chamber, at the point where the lichen glowed. Ginny was beside him, equally stunned by the suddenness of their arrival back in the normal world.

'C... crumbs!' she stammered. 'That was weirdly, weirdly, weird.'

Leo leaned back against the stone and remembered the vision.

'Neptune offers a kind sleep,' he said.

'I know,' Ginny agreed. 'Wasn't it all...'

'Don't say weird again,' Leo said, 'because, yes, it was weird, and it was amazing, too.'

He put his hand into his inside pocket and felt the tin lid, safe, light, and cool.

'We found The Way,' Ginny beamed. 'We *found* The Way! They're just the same as before, aren't they, Gido and Maria and the Grolchen? Oh, I wish I could've brought the Grolchen back. He'd be a great friend for Basil.'

A snuffling sound made them turn. Basil was scrambling back through the undergrowth beneath the holly tree. He emerged and shook himself. Then, tail wagging, he joined them by the stones, and settled down at Ginny's side. His ears pricked, as though he was listening to their conversation.

'Clever dog,' Ginny said, cuddling him. 'You found them for

us.'

'He did,' Leo nodded. 'I wonder how he got here. D'you think the Grolchen called him again.'

Ginny shrugged. 'No idea. What do we do now, Leo?' Ginny asked. 'What will you do with the brooch? Have you still got it?'

'Yes,' Leo said. 'It's in my pocket. I would've liked to ask them exactly what to do. Why couldn't we stay a bit longer and find out more?'

Ginny got up, shook the damp from her anorak and put it back on. 'It must be something to do with time-slips, like last time. We can't choose how long we stay. It just happens.' Then she looked serious. 'You should hide it. They'll come after us, looking for it.'

'Hiding it won't help,' Leo said. 'They'll come after us, just the same. You heard what Gido said. I think we do what we did last time. We don't wait for them to come after us. We go after them. We get them near water that connects to the sea, and we let things happen.'

He got to his feet and walked around the burial chamber one more time, hoping for inspiration.

'Come on. I'm starving,' Ginny said, looking at her watch.

'Okay.' Leo stroked the lichen covered stone. 'It's a magic place, isn't it?'

'Yes it is,' she agreed, heading off toward the gate, with Basil trotting happily behind her. 'But, I've had enough for today. I hope we've got a good tea waiting for us.'

★ ★ ★

Waiting for them, in fact, was not only a good tea, but a small surprise. Ginny's mother had arrived to visit. She had, she told them, brought Basil with her for an outing, because he seemed to be missing Ginny.

'No sooner had I arrived,' she told them, 'than off he goes. I shouted him to come back but he just vanished. Izzy said not to worry, he'd probably followed you.'

She laughed and ruffled Basil's coat. He laid at her feet, tongue lolling, and a happy look in his beady eyes.

'And she was right, wasn't she?' Ginny grinned, wondering why her mother had come.

'Your mum's been a bit worried about you,' Izzy said. 'You know how oddly you were behaving, getting drunk at your grandma's funeral, for example?'

Leo stared. 'Did you do that?' he asked Ginny, before he could stop himself.

She shrugged. 'A bit,' she admitted.

She leaned over her mum, who sat on the window seat, and gave her a big hug.

'I'm fine Mum, honestly. Leo and I are having a really good time.'

Her mum clasped her hand. 'That's all I want to know. Oh, yes, there was one other thing. Your library book. That odd young man from the library has been round about four times. Someone else has ordered it, and you should have taken it back weeks ago. I couldn't find it in your room, and I was going to telephone you, to ask where it was. Then I thought, no, she'll have it with her, and I thought to myself, I'll go and fetch it. It wasn't such a nice day, rainy, of course, but wouldn't let that put me off. An afternoon out at Newport would be just lovely, I told myself. The sun actually came out for a bit, and I have enjoyed seeing Izzy and everything. This house is wonderful and I get here so rarely, and the view is great.'

Her mother was known in the family for her unstoppable monologues, though they could be confusing for someone like Leo, exposed to them suddenly.

He was astonished by the avalanche of words, but he knew from the look on Ginny's face that the odd young man from the library had other motives than persuading her to give up her book for an anxious reader.

'What library book?' she demanded.

'I wrote it down,' her mother said, diving into her handbag. 'I wrote it down, because you know how sometimes words get mixed up. I'm always doing it and it is such a nuisance because, somehow, between there and here, words can tangle themselves into many different... oh yes, here it is. *A Dangerous War*. It's a history book, isn't it dear? I think he said it was a history book.'

Ginny frowned and glanced at Leo, who raised his eyebrows. In the same moment, they both understood who the persistent caller at her mother's house was, and the sinister threat implied in the message she had brought.

'He's got me mixed up with someone else,' Ginny blurted. 'I took all my books back ages ago.'

'Why did you think he was odd?' Leo asked.

'Something funny in the eyes,' Ginny's mother said. 'I've seen him before somewhere, but can't recall where.'

Both Leo and Ginny knew very well where, but neither said a word.

★ ★ ★

Later, after Ginny's mother and Basil had gone, and tea was over, Leo and Ginny sat together on the sea wall and watched the boats.

'Funny how things fit together,' Ginny said. 'My mum coming today; and Basil taking us through that hedge, and him being there at the right moment, it's almost as though...' She scratched her head and looked at Leo. 'Don't you think so?'

'Like being led along,' Leo said. 'I know exactly what you mean. That postcard thing was what got me, it really did. It's impossible to believe how that worked, whatever Gido says.'

'I only feel safe here because we're near the sea,' Ginny shivered. 'I'm really glad I wasn't at home when *he* came looking for me.'

'Somehow, we have to get them here,' Leo said looking up at the sky, wondering whether there were any large black birds in the vicinity. He couldn't see any, but he had an uneasy feeling that they would not take long to come and take a look, only to head back and report to the Dreamstealers.

'I think we head back to Cilgerran, to the castle,' he said eventually.

'No!' Ginny cried. 'I'm not going back there. If we do go there, they've got the whole parliament of rooks on their side. We wouldn't stand a chance.'

'Any other ideas?' he asked, knowing she was right.

'I do have one,' she said, 'but you won't like it any more than I like the idea of going back to the castle.'

'What?' he asked.

'I was thinking about that boy, Bos whats-his-name. We could go to see him, he might know something.'

Chapter 9

DREAMS AND SCHEMES

LEO WOKE SUDDENLY. He had been dreaming, and the dream had filled him with a dread that lingered, even when he sat up and saw familiar surroundings and had forgotten the dream itself. Now, as he tried to recollect the detail of it, he couldn't remember it at all.

He squinted at his watch. The time was 3.35. He looked again, to check the time, because bright silver light poured into the room and it was almost like dawn. Curiosity made him slip from bed, tiptoe to the window and lift back the curtain, to see where it came from. Above the sea an enormous full moon hung. Below, lit by the fierce whiteness of its uncanny glow, the tiny harbour glittered like fairyland.

He gazed at it, spellbound. It looked like a different world, every bit etched perfectly; all as clear as day and yet cloaked around with a dark night sky, peppered with stars.

On the surface of the sea, small ripples and waves picked up the light and shadow, and a huge face, formed on the water, seemed to look straight at Leo.

'Neptune,' he breathed.

For some unknown reason, he thought about Mrs Hallett. As though with this he had opened a box, and the contents had revealed themselves, he remembered the dream.

Mrs Hallett had been chasing him. Her eyes were the eyes of a Dreamstealer, and her hands were bony talons, which reached out, growing ever closer to him as he ran for cover, for help, for escape. A brave corner of him had taken control, and turning, he had faced his pursuer, holding out the brooch like a talisman. He had said some words, strange words that he knew but had never spoken, commanding her to leave him alone. He couldn't remember the words themselves, but he knew they meant something like, 'I know you. I see you.'

Strangely, he knew that this monster with the crazed eyes and the grasping talons wasn't Mrs Hallett at all. It was a Stealer in her shape. The effect of his words was to make the false Mrs Hallett stop and draw back, but then she began to rant and scream, and when Leo turned away from her, she spat at him repeatedly. The spittle had hit him like hailstones. Then he had woken.

He felt a draught of fear as the memory of that nightmare returned and he realised what it had shown him. The Stealer not only stole dreams, but could now use the shapes of those whose dreams he owned. He could use Mrs Hallett because he owned her dreams and knew her. He could turn into a rook because he had somehow conquered them. He could masquerade as anyone he had emptied of their live heart, their inner life. The drunk on the street in Cilgerran was another unfortunate victim. There were thousands of them, everywhere, all over the world, emptied, hollowed out by the fire still burning inside the Stealer from being boiled in the Cauldron of the Undead. Leo had occasionally considered that, since the Stealer could change shape, he might appear as Ginny, or as his mother, or anyone else he knew well, and trick him that way. It was an idea that always left him feeling sick and defeated. He knew now that the dream was a message telling him this couldn't happen. The Stealer's powers were limited, after all. A Stealer could only take the shape of those whose dreams he had taken.

The small surge of relief this brought was followed by a heavy sigh at the thought of the inevitable battle ahead. The Stealer had penetrated Leo's dream, and when he came to think about it, it even seemed that it had happened under that huge white moon. He watched the shadowy face come and go on the sea, and wondered what else there was in the dream that might help him. A light tap on his door shook him back to normality. Then, Ginny's head came round the door.

'Oh thank goodness, you are awake,' she whispered.

She was wearing rumpled yellow pyjamas and her hair stuck out in a damp mess. Leo thought how young she looked. It made him more determined than ever to be the one who decided what they did next. She came in and closed the door gently behind her.

She said, 'I'm too hot to sleep and I can't stop thinking about everything. I'm glad you're awake, too. Are you looking at the moon?'

Leo nodded, and turned back to gaze at the shining night world outside.

'It's so bright,' Ginny said, joining him by the window. 'Oh, look at all the boats and the water, everything is silvery and kind of unreal.' They watched the scene in silence for a few minutes. 'I keep wondering what's coming next,' Ginny admitted, eventually.

'Well, I can only tell you what *isn't* coming next,' Leo said. 'We're not going back to Narberth to look for Bos. Even if we could get him here, which I hate the thought of, the Stealers wouldn't follow him because they're scared of the sea, and Neptune.'

He looked back at the sea. The face that had seemed to look up at him from the smooth surface of the water had gone. Perhaps he had imagined it. '...so there's no point,' he finished.

'They came to Cilgerran, and that's not far from the sea,' Ginny argued.

'It's not *on* the sea, though, like we are here,' Leo pointed out. 'I guess they were desperate to get the brooch, and because the castle is so high and well up-river from the sea, they took a risk. I still think that's the best place to go. They may not know we have the brooch. They may still be there, looking for it. If we could chuck them over the edge...'

'Leo!'

'What else are we supposed to do?' Leo cried impatiently. 'Do we wait for them to do it to us? Do you want to be turned into a zombie like them, or end up bad-tempered and horrible for the rest of your life, like Mrs Hallett's going to be, or like my mum and your dad were, when they got caught by him? Remember what that was like?'

'Of course I remember it.' Ginny said, 'but I don't expect you to be so casual and say, "Let's just chuck them over the edge," as though it's easy. Anyway, I'm sure they do know we've got the brooch, because of the birds that followed us to The Way.'

'Not necessarily!' Leo said. 'You can't jump to conclusions. They were following us, yes. But they've been following us ever since we got here.'

'So?' Ginny's voice had risen. 'If we go and find that boy, go to Narberth where it all started...'

'I don't want his help. Why do you?' Leo asked, cutting her off in the middle of her sentence.

'I don't know! I just think that's where we should go!' cried Ginny. 'I don't know why! It just seems obvious.'

'Not to me,' Leo said stubbornly.

Their voices had grown louder in argument than they'd realised, and the door behind them opened, to show Izzy, in a long blue robe, looking at them with a patient but weary expression.

'What's going on?' she asked.

'Couldn't sleep,' replied Ginny.

'Try,' said Izzy, pointing to Ginny's room. 'Back to bed.'

Ginny shrugged and went from the room without argument.

'We were just looking at the moon,' she said as she left.

When she had heard the door to Ginny's room close, Izzy gave Leo a long, meaningful look. Leo wondered how much she had overheard.

'I hope you haven't forgotten, Leo, that you're supposed to be calming her down, not scaring her to death,' she said. She didn't wait for an answer. She just walked out, closed the door and returned to her room.

Leo sat a little longer at the window, feeling he'd been told off for something that wasn't his fault. It made him feel uncomfortable. He hated the thought that Izzy might think he was deliberately scaring Ginny. A cloud had come over the moon and a cool thread of air came through a small gap round the window. Leo closed the curtains and climbed back into his bed.

He sat up, his pillow behind his back, and began to think of ways to pursue the Stealers without getting Ginny involved. Surely, if they knew that it was he alone who had the brooch, and that Ginny was no threat at all to them, they might leave her alone and concentrate on him.

He went back to the window, pulled the curtain aside and looked again for Neptune's face. Gido's words, '*Choose your time, watch the moon and all that…*' flashed back into his mind. Then, from his buried memory of the last encounter with the Keepers, he remembered Gido explaining to him that, when the planet Neptune and the full moon came together in a certain way, they could provide a 'time-slip', opening up the wormholes through which the Keepers could enter into the real world. It was the only time they had any power to change things, to take real action; whereas, if they came through on the 'outer circle', as Gido and the Grolchen had done at Cilgerran, they could help, but not *be* there. The image of Neptune's face under the full moon meant that this was an appropriate time for him to take action. He was sure of it.

'In the morning, even though I can't see the moon, it will still be full, and Neptune will still be out there on the ocean. I can meet the Keepers at Carreg Coetan. I can summon them with the brooch. I know it was the brooch that brought Basil, I'm sure it was. I was carrying the brooch in my dream, and I held the Stealer back with it. Now, the Keepers can come through and help us.' Leo was happy in the knowledge that the words he needed would come to him when he needed them. He only had to open his mouth and they would emerge.

The thought suddenly struck him that he could go now. He wouldn't be able to sleep now, even if he tried. When he was sure that Ginny and Izzy were asleep, he would go. With the brooch in his pocket, he would be invincible. The passing cloud had gone and it was nearly as light as day outside. He wouldn't even need a torch. If he went alone, and brought the Keepers into the real world, maybe he could keep Ginny away from any potential danger.

Half an hour passed before he trusted that the others were sleeping. He dressed quickly, pulling on a fleece and jeans over his pyjamas and, after making a final check that he had the brooch in his pocket, he tiptoed out into the night.

The front door made a small click as he closed it.

He held his breath, but there was no sound from within. No voice called him, telling him to get back to bed. For a moment, he almost wished there had been one. Standing outside, alone, it didn't seem quite the adventure it had seemed while he was still lying in bed, thinking about it in safety. He wished Ginny was with him, and wondered whether he should go back and get her.

He chased the idea away. It would never do to involve her. If he got into trouble from Izzy for doing what had to be done, it would only be he who was punished. He shouldn't drag Ginny in.

He set off at a good pace. The complete emptiness of the streets, bathed in the silver light of the moon, was eerie. He tried not to think about what could go wrong, and reasoned that, as long as he stayed close to the sea and was ready to run if he spied anything like a Stealer, all would be well.

From the lane, he turned down the path toward the burial chamber. On either side were the bungalows, shrouded in darkness, but gleaming softly in the moonlight. The place looked different from in daylight. Somehow, the roofs looked higher, bumpier, more uneven, and the shadows under trees, behind hedges and fences, were black and threatening. With a jolt, he realised what was odd about those roofs, what made them look so uneven and so tall.

Looking like a true parliament, in uniform ranks, facing each other, with a path between them, silent rows of rooks sat, up on the tiles. Their eyes glittered. Their feathers shone blue-black. Their heads moved in unison, following Leo's footsteps.

Between him and the stones, there were hundreds of them. If they ambushed and attacked him, they could tear him to pieces.

Leo's first panicky thought was that they were waiting for him; that amongst them the Stealers were hiding, and an attack was indeed their intention, but reason took over. No one, not even Leo himself, had known that he was going to come here in the middle of the night. It had been a spontaneous decision. The birds had not so much as flapped at him, and he'd walked some way along the lane before he noticed them.

They appeared to be watching, but there was no sign of activity amongst them, and what better opportunity could there be to catch him than here, on the path, where he was hemmed in on either side?

He braced himself and, putting his hand into his pocket, he fingered the brooch. There was nothing left now to remind him of its wonderful powers; it was an old tin lid. No warm glow of changing sensation came from it. It was inert, asleep.

Leo took this as a good sign. If he was in big danger, if the Stealers really were amongst the rooks, and were instructing them, the brooch would have given him some warning.

Just then, he heard what sounded like musical notes, and he saw the birds turn their heads and look, not at him, but towards the burial chamber. There was a small light, beside the stones. It expanded gradually and seemed to consist of threads of light that wove themselves together into a ball, like wool. Leo, who had reached the end of the path, could clearly see what was happening. He watched in suspense and disbelief. Within the light, a figure moved; it was like a picture in a fire. Leo caught his breath, for he knew who it was.

It was the Grolchen, who, with a smile that almost reached his pricked ears, was tuning his Slop-Dinger, the peculiar instrument, somewhere between a violin and a keyboard, on which he played an accompaniment to his twin-faced howling. He had, as Leo well knew, won contests with this novel form of music, in many regions of Dreamworld, and was known to be amongst the very best at it.

The rooks, Leo realised, were not here to chase him, but had come together to listen to the Grolchen. This was a thought that, although it might seem to be ridiculous, made him feel considerably less afraid. If the rooks liked the Grolchen, that made the situation even better. Neptune, the Moon, twin-faced howling, stones and lights, all took Leo's thoughts and memories straight back to the circle at Gors Fawr, and his first visit to Dreamworld, that strange place, so like, yet unlike, the real world.

Hearing a noise behind him, Leo turned swiftly, hand on the brooch, and was astonished to see Gido standing beside him. He knew it was Gido, although he was not wearing his fancy waistcoat and old fashioned morning coat, which was how Leo thought of him. Instead, he was wearing a modern polo shirt and trousers. Maria was there too, without an apron or a funny bun on the top of her head. They both looked like anybody's respectable grandparents.

'We are in your world, Leo,' Gido said, with a nod of approval.

'We were looking forward to seeing you later today, but you have caught us unawares. The Grolchen is about to play for these poor birds, who have been affected by the Dreamstealers. They are anxious to reclaim their own power. In normal circumstances, they think as one, and move as a tightly knit group. The Dreamstealer has caused enormous splits between them. Grolchen will use sound, twin-faced of course, to restore their harmonious balance.'

'How did they know to come here?' Leo asked in confusion.

'Grolchen met some of their number on the outer circle, when he came to you at the castle. Distressed, I think would be the best word to describe their condition. He told them he would, when he could, come through to them with something restorative. They know the heaven's movements. They came in hope, and they will be rewarded.'

'That's amazing,' Leo said, gazing at the spectacle, remembering how, when he came out of the tunnel from the dungeon, he had thought the birds had been upset.

Now, amazingly, they were here as an eager audience.

'He'll have to be a dog tomorrow,' said Maria, watching the Grolchen. 'Just for the day. Till we slip back.'

'You don't sound the same,' Leo said to her, 'and you don't look the same, either of you.'

'We're in your world. We fit in better,' laughed Maria.

'I came to see if I could use the brooch to bring you through,' Leo said.

'No need. We were ready as soon as the moon touched its quincunx with the retrograde Neptune,' Gido said.

'You're really here to help us?' Leo's relief was huge.

'Ssh!' said Maria. 'Listen and marvel.'

The Grolchen began to play. The sound of the slop-dinger floated into the air. Each single, resonant note drifted up and up, and seemed to be visible, to take on the colours of the night, the silver of the moon, the dark blue of the sky, the fiery white of the stars. Just as Leo, his mouth wide, seemed to rise himself with the sounds, and be floating in the leaves of the trees, high in the air, the Grolchen began to sing.

From one side of his cat-like face came a murmuring, rhythmic undertone, accompanied by a dark, almost evil leer, and from the other side came a high falsetto, and a facial expression that spoke purity and innocence.

It was riveting and it was hair-raising. How, Leo wondered, could two sounds coming from one throat, so strange, so opposite, be woven together to create such magical music? How could the Grolchen, whose vocabulary was limited to three short words, be able to communicate such subtlety, such invention, such wickedness, such glorious fun, from sounds the like of which Leo had never heard before?

The rooks, Leo could see from the corner of his eye, were as mesmerised as he was. Was it possible that the Grolchen was really healing them with sound? Leo remembered once asking the Keepers what they really looked like, and being told by Gido, *'We don't look like anything. We're made of sound.'*

The music wrapped around him. The night seemed filled with it. For those minutes, Leo stood listening, rapt, his fears calmed. When it ended, the Grolchen took several bows, in response to a rapturous flapping of wings from the rooks. His finest asset, his hairy rear, which always looked to Leo as though a lion's head had been put on at the wrong end, waved cheerfully at his audience, as, with the final note still ringing round the sky, the rooks took off in a great flock and headed away across the estuary.

The dead silence of the night that followed the birds' departure made Leo wonder for the first time what the people in the bungalows made of it.

'They live beside the stones.' Gido said, as if he had read Leo's mind. 'They see and they don't see. They hear and they don't hear.'

Leo wasn't sure he knew what Gido meant, but there was certainly no sign of irate neighbours complaining about the noise. Leo yawned. It was still night-time and he had not slept.

The light around the Grolchen faded, he disappeared from view, and in his place, a dog appeared, a large, rough-coated dog that looked remarkably like Rolf, who had been Basil's best friend.

'Was the dog still in Dreamworld while Grolchen was playing?' asked Leo. 'I thought he was here, like you are.'

'How could he take form as a Grolchen here?' asked Maria. 'You don't have them in your world, do you? Nearest thing he can be is a dog. Although, some do come as cats, and some come as other creatures. They can't be human of course.' She said this as though it was something for which to be thankful. 'Whichever world he's in, if he isn't playing music, he's up to mischief,' she finished.

Leo was about to ask for more detail, but Gido cut in. 'Go to Narberth, Leo,' he said. 'We'll see you there.'

Next, all three disappeared, and Leo was back at the start of the path, looking down between the bungalows, their roofs empty of rooks, as though time itself had gone backwards, but time had moved on. The light was changing, and dawn traced pale fingers across the sky.

Leo turned and began to walk back to Izzy's. There was no more to be done for now. Morning would see things moving again, of that he was positive. Whatever the Keepers had in store for the Dreamstealers, Leo would do his best to help them make it happen. He felt hungry and thought about breakfast and hot coffee as he trudged along, his hands sunk deep in the pockets of his fleece. Tiredness made him feel cold, and there was a freshening breeze from off the sea.

Two fishermen, preparing for work, nodded to him as he passed, as though it was perfectly normal for a boy of his age to wander about at 5 o'clock in the morning.

★ ★ ★

Bos was on tenterhooks. His wealthy friend had reappeared and, with a casual mockery that gave no appearance of sincerity, had apologised for the misunderstanding at the castle.

'It should not have happened,' he said dismissively. 'We became confused by the appearance of those other youngsters. We thought, perhaps, you were working with them and against us. We did not intend to imprison a colleague, which was how we had come to regard you. I took no pleasure in propelling you down the steps on the end of my boot. It was purely functional. You seemed to be a traitor. It was only later that we realised you had been unaware that the others were coming that day. We, too, of course, expected you but not them. It was a confusing day. I have a large wad of cash in my pocket. You smile as we speak. Can we not be friends, lad?'

He gazed at the boy, in that strange compelling way he had, and Bos could not refuse him. Bos's heart lifted, and he felt rosy, golden and loved. Moments later, he shivered and felt an emptiness sweep through him that made him reach out his arms and lean on a nearby wall. He didn't really believe a word, but it didn't matter. He was enthralled and terrified to such an extent by the figure that faced him, he would have agreed to anything.

They were on the top lane, behind Narberth's main street, where Bos had been wandering in the hopes of spotting an open rear door to a shop, where he could swiftly and secretly pocket something handy. The man had suddenly appeared in front of him, just as though it was an appointed meeting.

This, thought Bos, was how it always was with the man. He would appear from nowhere, and then Bos was trapped. He couldn't resist the promise, the dream, the most wonderful moment of all that came with seeing the man, but as soon as he sank into it with elation and anticipation, it turned to a barren desert of sense and feeling; a drought, a famine, a disaster, a war zone.

Before he knew it, his mind filled with any, or all, of these. The only thing to do was to carry out instructions, because that meant there would be money, and more money, and that was the one thing to make it all feel better in time.

Bos felt the desperate mood swings, but didn't understand how or why they happened. He only knew that he had to obey. He didn't know the identity of the man that stood before him. He didn't recognise him, as Leo would have, as one of the Stealers. Who the 'we' were that the man talked about he had no idea, but he knew, looking into those dread, magnetic eyes, that he had no choice but to do as he was told.

The meeting was over in less than a couple of minutes, and, having extracted Bos's co-operation, the man turned and disappeared. Bos blinked. He was alone, except for a wire-haired black cat that was stalking away from him.

Once the man had gone, Bos felt a mixture of relief and excitement. He had a mission. He wasn't sure how he could carry it out, but if he succeeded, Leo and his sister would be like him. That would mean he would have friends like himself. If the man could only claim them, gaze at them, show them the ecstatic dream-world that only he could unveil for them, and then make them his servants, wonder of wonders he, Bos, would have brought them there.

★ ★ ★

It was after nine o'clock when Ginny persuaded herself to knock on Leo's bedroom door and wake him. She'd been up an hour, been to the shop for bread and a newspaper, and been followed home by a stray dog that looked like her old friend Rolf, but reminded her very much of the Grolchen.

Leo blinked at her from over the edge of his duvet. He hadn't meant to fall asleep, but had been overcome by tiredness as soon as his head hit the pillow. The sleep had been deep and dreamless. The events of the early hours, like a distant dream, came back to him. He rubbed his eyes and pushed his hands through his tousled hair.

'You were right, Ginny' he said. 'We go to Narberth.'

'A dog followed me. It's sitting on the step. Izzy let me feed it. It's...'

'Like Rolf,' Leo said, cutting off her words.

★　★　★

Rolf 2, alias the Grolchen, was not to be shaken by the mere prospect of a bus ride. He jumped on the bus, behind the two children, with all the enthusiasm of a guard dog. They had no choice but to pay his fare. He lay at their feet, his tail thumping cheerfully.

Izzy had been mystified by their sudden announcement that they were going to Narberth for the day.

'But why?' she asked. 'They're forecasting a nasty storm for later. You'd be better staying here.'

'We really want to go,' Leo said. 'I want to get a couple of things I wish I'd brought from home. My camera, for instance. It didn't occur to me to bring it,' he said. 'Besides, Ginny doesn't know Narberth that well. It'll be good fun.'

He wondered how he was able to lie so easily. Fun was not at all what this was about. Moreover, it occurred to him that, had Izzy seen the dog jumping on board the bus with them, she would have had even more to wonder at.

★　★　★

Bos turned down the hill and came onto the main street. In a moment of shock, followed by wicked satisfaction, ahead of him, he saw Leo and Ginny getting off a bus. This would be easier than he'd hoped. The man had said he would wait until Bos brought Ginny and Leo to the Pendaran café. He had been most specific about the location.

Pendaran was a run-down shack on the edge of Narberth, where lorry drivers and men on motorbikes met. It was rough and not a suitable place for children, in the normal way of things. Bos knew it wouldn't be easy to lure them there, but he couldn't protest to the man. He'd imagined he would have to go to Newport, find them there and, on some pretext, persuade them to come to Narberth. An emergency, he would say. Leo's mother had sent him to find them. But he didn't have to do any of that. They were here! All he had to do was get them to the café.

He wondered whether the man had known they were coming to Narberth. How long would he have waited? Days? Weeks? Bos struggled vainly to think straight, and then, he gave up. How the man would reward him for his success was more important. Perhaps he would have enough money to run away to Cardiff, or London, to buy his way to a rich and comfortable life of idleness.

He thought about the money the man had given to him, the previous time. Where had it gone? He had no memory of spending it, enjoying it, and his mind went blank when he thought about it. Had it been real at all, or, had he dreamt it? No matter, not now. He would think about that some other time. For now, he had more important things on his mind. He quickened his pace to catch up with his targets.

★ ★ ★

'I hope we're doing the right thing,' Leo said, looking down at Rolf 2, who was jogging on the spot. 'He's not terribly dog-like for a dog is he?'

'I bet he's a...'

'Wayfinder,' finished Leo, as the dog suddenly took off like lightning down the main street, and disappeared.

'We have to find him,' Ginny cried.

She turned as she spoke, tossing her hair back and tucking it behind her ear. Suddenly, out of the corner of her eye, she saw Bos. Her eyes widened and Leo glanced round to see what had caught her attention. They both froze for a split second; when they saw him coming toward them, they sensed the aura of bleak despair that hung around him, reminding them instantly of the Stealer.

'He's been with them again,' Leo muttered. 'They know we're here.'

Ginny shivered. Bos tried to give them a friendly grin. It was a twist of the lips that had more of the sinister than the cheerful in it. Leo was overcome with a breathtaking awareness of how often he had seen the aura before and not known it for what it was. Just before he spoke to Bos, Leo could have recited the names of everyone he had ever met, who the Stealers must have touched.

Gido had told him the Dreamstealer's curse was an 'infection' that passed from one person to another. It scared him. Mostly it scared him because he knew that his ability to see it was due to the brooch, which now felt warm in his pocket. Without it, he would never have known he'd seen it. Then, he had a sudden panicky thought. Could Bos infect him and Ginny, without them even having to meet with the Stealers?

He dismissed the thought instantly. Bos, of all people, couldn't persuade him of anything. He waved at Bos, and started to run in the opposite direction.

'Got to catch the dog,' he yelled.

'I'll 'elp yer,' cried Bos, chasing after him, knowing that they were headed towards the road out of town, and the Pendaran café.

Chapter 10

SCRAP AND SKIRMISH

THE PENDARAN CAFÉ was no more than a big tin shed. Its green painted walls were peeling and rusting. Around it, on the waste ground used as a car park, were piles of ancient scrap. Three large trucks, which were parked on it, competed for space with broken-down engines, long-dead cars and heaps of tyres. Outside, on the road in front, stood a row of gleaming motor cycles, whose owners obviously didn't want to risk the oily puddles and obstacles the car park offered.

Ginny, who had arrived first, viewed it with a frisson of fear. She had run as fast as she was able, trying to keep Rolf in sight but, at the last corner, she had lost sight of him. There were no other buildings on this long stretch of road, and she could see across the fields on either hand. Reason said he must have gone into this uninviting café. She stood, uncertain whether to go further; something was telling her it was not safe to enter, something else goading her on.

Before she could take a step, pandemonium broke loose inside the building. She could hear the sounds of shrieking, cursing and, above the voices, a terrible roaring noise, as though a lion had arrived out of the African jungle and was furious at where it had found itself. Men began to fall out of the doors. In their haste to get away, they stumbled over each other in order to get to their machines. While helmets were crammed madly on heads, and leather jackets struggled into, the bikes were kicked into life, and the bikers took off at alarming speed. A large sign that proclaimed, *'Our Pies Are Heavenly. Come In And Try One'* was knocked to the ground in the stampede.

The truck drivers followed, diving into their cabs, with half-eaten bacon sandwiches in their hands, as though the hounds of hell were after them. In seconds, they were screeching out of the place on two wheels.

Ginny watched, open-mouthed. After the noise of the vehicles died away, the only sound was the deep, frightening roar, which still came from the café, even though it appeared to have emptied of people. She moved gingerly toward the doors, just as Leo arrived, followed by a panting Bos.

'What's going on?' Leo asked, having seen with some amazement a number of motor bikes swerving and wobbling past, heading away. 'I lost you.'

'I don't know,' Ginny said. 'There's an animal in the café. Listen to that racket! It couldn't be Rolf, could it?'

'Only if he can't do proper dog noises,' said Leo, 'which I guess is possible. But if it is him, what's he up to?'

'He came this way. I know he did,' Ginny said. 'I lost sight of him, and there was no sign of him on the road, or in the fields.'

'We'd better take a look inside,' Leo said, sounding braver than he felt.

He stepped into the gloomy interior. It took his eyes a moment to adjust, but when they had, he saw that Ginny had been right. The dreadful noise came, indeed, from the un-doglike throat of Rolf, alias the Grolchen, He was standing on top of a man, who was pinned to a table by Rolf's huge, hairy paws. The man writhed and struggled, attempting to free himself.

The Grolchen danced on his back, roaring like a lion. The man screamed and fought. The Grolchen threw back his head, roared even louder, and executed a firm polka step, up and down the man's spine. The noise that came from the animal's throat was the most appalling sound Leo and Ginny had ever heard. It made their insides turn to water.

Bos, who was hanging around outside, timidly looking in, had already decided he was going no further.

Then, the Grolchen saw Leo and Ginny, and the sheer terror on their faces made him stop what he was doing. The roar descended to a quieter growl, which still sounded threatening but was less alarming to the children.

'Get him OFF!' screamed the man, making a great effort to draw up his legs and kick out.

Bos, programmed to obey, began to walk into the café, from his safe spot outside, with no more control over his actions than a puppet. He had to help the man. After all, the man was waiting for Bos and, of course, Leo and Ginny. Then, Bos registered the dog on the man's back; it growled back at him with bared teeth, and he froze. For a split second, as he looked at it, he saw again the dungeon tunnel, and the peculiar animal, Leo's friend, that had appeared and disappeared. He thought, 'I know that dog. It isn't a dog. It's that hairy monster that was in the dungeon.'

Even though an ordinary mad dog was terrifying enough, Bos knew that this beast could do magic, and so it was even more dangerous. He wasn't sure he wanted to do anything at all to help the man.

Ginny and Leo watched. They knew who the man was, even

though they had not yet seen his eyes. There was a faint, but familiar, smell hanging in the air, and, once before, they had seen the Grolchen riding on the back of a Dreamstealer.

The man stopped struggling, and seemed to be taking breath. Grolchen growled on, standing firm, his back legs on the man's shoulders, and his front feet on his buttocks, facing Leo and Ginny.

'Whose is that dog?' A woman's sharp voice came from somewhere behind the counter. When the question was answered by silence, the voice continued, 'Get the damn thing out of here. It's scared my customers to death, and if you can't make it behave, you should have it put down. There was that poor gentleman, sitting, pleasant as you please, having a cup of tea, and that great thing vaults over the tables and lands on him like a ton of potatoes. I've never seen anything like it. And that noise! For heaven's sake! What's it crossed with? A cow?' No one answered. 'I'll ring the police if you don't get it out of here,' the voice continued.

Leo decided he must act. The customers were gone and the café owner had a perfect right to be angry, but Leo had no idea how the Dreamstealer would behave if released. He stepped forward.

'Rolf,' he said, reaching out a hand to stroke the animal, 'down, boy.'

The growling stopped. The dog seemed to lose about two stone in weight as it jumped lightly to the ground. On the man's back, it had looked huge, towering, and gigantic, but now, it simply looked like a large dog.

The Dreamstealer lifted himself up and climbed from the table. He brushed his clothes down and pressed his hair back against his head. His face, skull-like, with its haunting eyes, stared back at them.

Ginny knew she must look anywhere but into his eyes. She watched his feet. Leo, remembering what he had done in his dream, held the brooch out in front of him. He also avoided the Stealer's eyes, looking instead at his hands. The brooch felt hot. Small flashes, almost too rapid for the eye, flickered across its surface. It was like watching a control panel, thought Leo, or a circuit board.

The Stealer's eyes narrowed, when he saw what Leo was holding, and Leo knew that, somehow, the brooch shielded him and rendered the Stealer incapable of attack.

'You have stolen something of ours,' he rasped.

Leo spoke to the man's chest. 'We dispute your claim,' he said, looking steadily ahead.

The Stealer smiled, as though he thought Leo a stupid child, who could not stand against him. Leo began to walk backwards towards the outer door, carefully avoiding the tables and chairs, holding the brooch between himself and the Stealer.

'We're leaving,' he said to Ginny. 'Bring Rolf.'

Rolf was already ahead of them. His tail was wagging and he was ready for whatever might come next. He bounded out into the street.

The woman came out from behind the counter and started to wipe down tables, keeping an eye on what was happening. Ginny followed Leo's example, moving towards the outside door, never taking her eyes from the man's feet. The Stealer stood and watched them go.

Bos didn't know what to do. All he could think was, that Leo shouldn't leave.

The man might not give him his money now.

'You said you'd pay me if I brought 'em, an' I did,' he whined. 'I couldn't stop that thing from jumpin' all over you. It wan't my fault.'

Leo and Ginny heard him. They paused. Both wanted to leave, but both wanted to listen to what Bos said. They had heard him, and were shocked. Had Bos really brought them here? What was he talking about?

When Bos looked hopefully at the Stealer, he felt the burn of hatred and contempt, as the dreaded eyes looked back at him. Bos looked down quickly, away from the man's face, terrified, knowing that, if he looked into his eyes any longer, he would see things he would rather not see. He shuffled his feet and began to walk away. The man reached out. His bony fingers laced in a vice-like grip around Bos's arm.

'Where are you going?' he hissed. 'I still need you. This place is where a valuable piece of property is destined to become mine. I have seen inside the dreams of others, I have calculated my power here by the movements of the heavens and the sea, I can change shape and time to utmost effect. I have done all these things here, in this place; and what happens? That hairy, vicious creature happens. But, never mind that. It's over. Now things can move on.'

Still he smiled at Bos, who stood like a rabbit caught in headlights. Leo knew, then, that he and Ginny were in a trap. The Stealer was smiling because he had something up his sleeve, or, more likely, outside the door. Leo heard a terrifying yelp come from somewhere outside, and then there was silence. He turned to see what was happening, and looked straight into the eyes of the second Dreamstealer, who stood on the threshold behind him. Leo felt as though he was falling, that his veins were turning to ice; his forehead was running with sweat. He wrenched his eyes away and leant against the nearest table for support.

'Where's Rolf?' shrieked Ginny, 'Where is he?'

She tried to run past the man in the doorway, but he stood firm, holding out his arms and filling the space.

'Going nowhere,' called the other one, who was still holding Bos by the arm. 'And don't waste your time trying to talk to him. He can't speak. He can't even think. I do it all for him. He came late from the Cauldron.' He laughed. 'He can steal your dreams, though. Oh yes, he can separate you from your soul. He can move through time and shift his shape. So, be wary of him, little one. Don't get him angry.'

Ginny turned on him. She tried looking at his ears. It was better than watching his feet, which meant keeping her head down and not seeing anything of what was going on, but it was uncomfortably close to his eyes. She dropped her eyes to his neck.

'Where is our dog?' she said, through clenched teeth.

'Not your dog,' the Stealer said. 'We know who he is. He's a self-appointed do-gooder from that stupid bunch who call themselves the Keepers. We know your relationship with them.'

'Where is he?' Ginny asked again.

'Gone home,' the Stealer said. 'Give to us what is ours, and you, too, may go home.'

'You're wasting your time,' Leo said.

He wondered where Gido and Maria were. Surely, since Gido had instructed him to come to Narberth, he and Maria should be here when they were needed.

'Time?' the Stealer queried. '*I* am wasting time? Not possible. Since I do not live within time, I can do what I like with it. You, on the other hand, may find yourself in a much less pleasant place in time, unless you give me what is ours.'

He turned to Bos. 'The brooch protects those two from me and my brother. We cannot wrestle them to the ground and snatch it from them, but you can, of course.'

Bos's face registered a 'get me out of here' expression. Leo stood head and shoulders taller than he did, and, like all bullies, he was a coward when it came to getting hurt.

The woman from behind the counter had stopped what she was doing and was looking on. A man came through a door from the kitchen and stood next to her. Leo couldn't see them clearly, their faces were in shadow, but something told him who they were.

'There'll be no fighting in my café,' the woman said. Turning to the man, she said, 'Phone the police.'

The Stealer turned and looked at the couple.

Leo's arm was beginning to ache with the strain of holding out the brooch, and, what was worse, it was growing heavier all the time. The flashes of electricity that passed across it had increased, and it was getting uncomfortably hot.

'Support my arm, Ginny,' Leo whispered. 'It's getting really hard to hold it still.'

Ginny put her arm under Leo's forearm, and clasped her hand firmly on to his.

'I keep thinking I should be able to do something with it,' Leo whispered to her. 'I thought spell words would, sort of, say themselves when we met him, but I can't think of any.'

The Stealer had walked across to look closer at the man and woman by the kitchen door.

'You!' he spat, after staring for a few moments. 'I might have known you'd turn up.' Then he smiled one of his dark smiles. 'You can't help them, and you know it,' he said. 'The brooch stops you from doing any act in this world, except to defend. I am not attacking anyone, as you see.'

He turned to Leo, pleased with himself. 'I don't suppose you knew that, did you? Surprised? Don't be. Watch!'

He prodded Gido in the chest. Gido drew himself up and brushed him off.

'Stop playing games,' he said. 'We know as well as you do the laws of Manawl's magic.'

The Stealer was enjoying himself. He returned to face Leo. 'What it comes down to is a fight between two boys,' he said. 'Your precious piece of history is no good to you, because, unlike us, you have no idea how to use it. Can you read Manawl's spells? No. Can you even begin to know how to access the power you hold in your hand? No. You are a small boy, an ignorant and useless small boy, but you may be able to put up a fight.'

He turned back to Bos, and nodded toward the man and the woman.

'Actors,' he said to him. 'Don't worry about them phoning the police. They're only actors.'

Bos looked no happier. Ginny was watching the movements of light across the brooch. She had become mesmerised, from the moment she had clasped Leo's hand which held it, and as she stood side on next to him, she couldn't help leaning in closer and watching the strange flashing lights. She had even begun to think that the sparks of light made some kind of sense. It was almost as if she could read it.

'*Imbyl, blaenweddi,*' she read aloud. '*Man... aw... ydd ...an...*'

'What?' Leo gasped. He had an inkling what the words meant, but he had no idea whether Ginny knew what she was saying.

'*Galwad... os gwelwch yn dda... fab Llyr,*' she continued, in a sing-song, creepy tone.

'I don't think...' Leo began.

'Do you know where we are?' Gido's voice interrupted him. 'We are, or would be, in a different time.'

'That's enough,' the Stealer snarled. 'We know where we are. In the halls of the palace of Arberth. So what? These pathetic fools will never unlock a time spell. We are here, in this century. Two boys will fight and our boy will win. He knows he must. It was said, when the brooch was lost, that it would be found at Arberth, at Manawl's home. For centuries, we thought it was here, but it wasn't. He lost it at Cilgerran, and *we* discovered it was there, and you jumped in to stop us because you heard gossip in Dreamworld. It was *ours* to find. No one else's. And it is fitting that it should come to us here. It is ours; not yours.'

Ginny was still reading from the brooch; she was in a trance-like state, as though she couldn't even hear the Stealer. Leo wondered whether she might be suffering from shock, or had such fright that it had turned her brain.

Her eyes were fixed on the brooch, and she was mouthing words in increasing volume and uttered in a sing-song way.

'Crydd parchedig
Rhyd wyn dilyn
Dewch, dewch,

Manawl,

Peid yr ymladd,

Manawl fab Llyr.'

As the last syllable passed her lips, the building shook.

'Stop her!' screamed the Stealer. 'Stop her! She is making an invocation. She is bringing him here. No! No!'

The café shook with such force, it seemed as if an earthquake had struck. Everything rocked, fell, bounced, and tumbled. There was a rushing sound, and a strong wind blew through the place, from end to end.

Ginny, holding on to a skidding chair, continued to sing, even though she was no longer looking at, or holding on to, the brooch. She repeated the same words as she had spoken the first time, but, somehow, longer bits were creeping in. To Leo, it sounded like when he tried to sing something and had forgotten the words, which came back as he sang. It seemed as if she sang from memory.

He crouched by the wall, holding on to an upright beam with one hand, still holding the brooch in the other. In his hand, as if by its own volition, the brooch turned itself toward him. Looking down at it, Leo saw a face looking back at him, a powerful, living face, with grey eyes that looked straight into Leo's own.

In shock, he flung it from him, and it hit the floor. Ginny leapt and scooped it up. The building shook again.

'Get it from her,' shrieked the Stealer to Bos. 'Jump on her. Grab it now, and we will all leave before…'

But Bos was unable to move. Overcome by fear, he was clinging to the counter as the building heaved. He didn't want to disobey the Stealer, who, legs astride, like a man on a ship riding the waves, was shaking his fist in a threatening manner. Bos ignored him; he knew something awful was happening. If it wasn't an earthquake, it might be a dinosaur coming up from the bowels of the earth. Something terrible was on its way, and even the Stealer could not persuade Bos to move.

Ginny was now holding out the brooch and still singing, despite the Stealer's howls of protest. This time, as the last word rang in the air, a man appeared, like a smoky apparition. The man looked steadily at each of the Stealers, who, in turn, seemed to shrink under his gaze. Then he looked at Ginny.

'So,' he said. 'You are the voice that called me.'

Ginny gazed back at him. He was the handsomest, most exciting, wonderful person she had ever laid eyes on, and *she* had brought him here. But from where?

He was not dressed in modern clothes. There was no attempt to 'fit in', in the way the Keepers and the Stealers had done. This man looked like a king from ancient times. He wore a simple gold band round his head, and around his shoulders was a long, dark green cloak. At the neck, it was fastened with a single gold pin.

He did not smile at her, but neither did he frown. He just looked at her, with calm grey eyes. She wasn't sure if he was pleased that she had called him, or not. Then, the man turned his eyes on Leo.

'Manawl,' Leo croaked, his throat dry.

The man bowed his head. 'So they call me,' he said.

'Have you come for your brooch,' Ginny asked, 'to fasten your cloak with?'

Manawl's eyes lit with humour as he shook his head.

'It is in the material world because that is where it was made. I cannot use it in Annwn. We are the watchers only. Earth magic belongs in your world,' he explained.

'Then, perhaps you can tell us how to use it,' Ginny said. 'It's not much good to us, unless we know what to do with it, is it?'

Leo was embarrassed for her. She was speaking to the ghostly King in a cheeky, familiar way that implied she had no idea of how important and powerful he was, but Manawl apparently did not mind.

'It seems that you are doing quite well without my help,' he said, 'but since you ask, I see no reason why I shouldn't assist you in some small way. I will tell you the words to open the book.'

He leaned down between the two of them, and whispered his secret. The Stealer beside Bos moved. He looked as though he was drunk. He took three unsteady steps toward the kingly apparition's back. Manawl turned, raised a hand in the air, and pointed toward the creeping figure, who stopped in his tracks, shaking from head to foot.

Manawl's eyes alighted on Bos, and lingered there for a few moments. Then, he turned and looked again at the second Stealer, who still stood guarding the door.

'Your time is almost come,' he said to him.

There was no response from the figure, but Leo heard a short cough from the corner where Gido and Maria stood. Manawl looked toward them.

'I had thought you wiser than to throw your problems onto children,' he said to them. 'However, now I have seen them, I understand. They are *Dewin Ifanc, Dethol.*' Gido and Maria looked at the floor, having been scolded.

Manawl turned back to the children.

'Do not call me again,' he said to Ginny. 'There are far more useful ways to use the brooch than to bring me all this way. Annwn is as far from your world as it is possible to be, and it was not an easy journey.'

Leo started mumbling an apology, but Manawl raised a hand to stop him.

'These dreamselves whom you are assisting,' he nodded toward Gido and Maria, 'have you guessed yet why they are so desperate for your help?'

He was smiling, as though he knew a secret, but he didn't wait for an answer. He was leaving. His voice was still there as his apparition dissolved.

'Your lives to us are like plays,' he was saying, 'like stories; as ours are to you. One day, you will know. All is revealed in time.'

With that, he dwindled into the air and disappeared.

'Get the brooch, boy!' The Stealer was shaking Bos.

Bos's tears spilled down his cheeks and dripped onto his sweatshirt. He had never seen a ghost before, and something about this particular one had scared him beyond reason. This was a good man, a holy man, somehow, and he had looked at him, Bos, with pity and love in his eyes. Bos tried to wipe away his tears with his sleeve, but he couldn't stop more coming. It was all too much for him.

'I don't want to do it,' he sobbed. 'It in't fair. You shoun't make me.'

'You will find out what I can make you do,' came the Stealer's harsh reply. 'If you cannot take the brooch from a mere girl, what use are you to us? Do it! Do it, or face the consequences.'

Bos had no option but to move toward Ginny. Fear and

automatic response worked together as he reached out and tried to grab the brooch from her, but his attempt was, after all, half-hearted, and Ginny jumped sideways, easily avoiding his reaching hand. Strengthened by the power Manawl had brought into the room, she glared at Bos.

'You wouldn't dare,' she flashed. 'Just you keep your distance from me, you creep!'

Leo narrowed his eyes and stared at Bos.

'You coward!' he said. 'You'll fight with a girl, but not with me? Give the brooch back to me, Ginny. Then see if he still wants it.'

Ginny was about to do as Leo asked, and pass it back to him, when she was struck by an idea. Manawl's voice was still in her ears. He had spoken directly to the Stealer at the door, the one Ginny suspected of hurting the animal she had come to think of as Rolf. She turned on him, and thrust the brooch out in front of her.

'Where is my dog?' she shouted at him. 'Where is my dog?'

She moved toward him, and, to her surprise, he began to stagger backwards, out of the doors. Once that man was through them, she turned to Leo. She could see the other Stealer moving toward him, pushing Bos in front of him.

'Come on!' she cried, tossing the brooch back to Leo, so that he could protect himself. It was a less than perfect throw, and a less than perfect catch.

Leo leapt, reached for it and missed. It landed, with a tinny clink, on the wooden floor, and rolled away from him.

In a split second, Gido and the Stealer dived toward it. The Stealer was nearer and, with a triumphant cry, he grasped it in his hand.

Gido groaned, and Maria put her head in her hands.

'We've lost,' she wailed.

'There is yet time to tip the scales,' Gido said. 'Leo…'

At that moment, Leo heard Ginny, who was already outside, give a blood-curdling scream. He didn't know which way to turn. The sight of the Stealer's cackling elation as he held aloft his prize, the disappointment on the faces of Gido and Maria, and the loss of the wonderful brooch that had made him feel so strong and chosen, made him feel sick, and a failure.

He longed to leap on the Stealer, kick his shins and make mincemeat of him, but, at the same time, he knew he had to run in answer to the screaming beyond the café door. He almost fell outside, and the first thing he saw was Rolf's body lying in the dust at the roadside. Then he saw that Ginny had thrown herself on the silent Stealer, and was beating him with her fists, whilst he fended her off. She was screaming at the top of her voice.

'You killed him! You killed him!'

The man lifted her in the air with one hand, as though he was about to throw her on to the roof of the café. Suddenly, the others were there. Gido and Maria, now released from the law of the brooch that had held them back from fighting, because the Stealer was attacking Ginny, joined Leo and, together, they leapt on him, struggling and fighting, holding him down. Ginny tumbled to the ground.

'Ow!' she screamed, but she was only bruised, and she quickly joined with the others in holding the Stealer down. He wrestled and began to change shape under their hands, grew bigger, fiercer, and, frighteningly, his teeth became like fangs.

156

'Take no notice,' Gido grunted to the children, while they were all still struggling to hold the Stealer. 'He's the same in the middle as he was before. It's an illusion. Close your eyes, if it scares you to look at him.'

Maria, who was a karate expert, aimed sharp kicks at the man's legs, and he dropped with a moan, his scary face changing yet again.

Leo, was clinging on to the Stealer's arm, trying to twist it up his back, when he saw the other Stealer emerge from the café, holding Bos by the arm, pulling him along.

'Look! Look!' Leo shouted. 'He's running off with the brooch, and he's got Bos.'

Gido turned to look, then brought his face up close to the captured Stealer, still struggling in their grasp, and said fiercely to him,

'He's leaving you. See? Your brother. So much for brotherhood. You are lost without him. Give up. Give up now.'

The Stealer, hearing this, seemed to wilt. He stared at the disappearing figures of Bos and the Stealer, as though he couldn't believe his eyes. He visibly shrank, and all resistance seemed to leave him.

Chapter 11

NEPTUNE'S TIDE

LEO COULD HEAR a siren growing louder, warning of a police car headed their way. He wondered who had called them. Maybe, it was the café owners, whom Gido and Maria had somehow replaced. It had only now occurred to him that there must have been someone else there, behind the counter, before the Keepers took over. He hoped that the car was on its way somewhere else, and would drive by and ignore them.

The Stealer had gone completely limp. Not only was he no longer fighting, it seemed as if he had lost the will to keep any shape other than his own.

Inside his suit, he had begun to shrink to his skeleton self, and the terrible, burnt, deathly smell that came from him seemed to be everywhere. The police did not drive by, as Leo had hoped, but stopped to see what was going on. One of them got out of the car, holding a handkerchief to his nose. For an awful moment, Leo thought he was going to come and take a closer look, but Maria forestalled him by calling across to him.

'Drunk again!' she shouted. 'What would you do with a man like this?'

'You've got a problem there, love,' he called back. 'We can do him for drunk and disorderly, but we're on a job right now. Anyway, it'd be better and cheaper for you if you can get him home.'

'Don't I know it,' she agreed.

'Is that dog yours?' shouted the other one, still sitting in the car, craning across to see as much as possible without getting out from behind the wheel.

Maria nodded.

'He looks as drunk as your old man,' he said. 'Get them home. Your kids'll give you a hand; save us wading in. We're looking for a gang of Hell's Angels, seen driving like the devil through town.'

'And now,' interrupted the other one, still holding the handkerchief firmly to his nose, 'we've to find where this foul stink's coming from. Smells like an abattoir on fire!'

With that, he jumped back into the car and they drove off.

'Thank goodness,' Maria said, watching them go. 'We'd have had a bit of a job explaining this.'

They looked down together at the crumpled heap on the ground.

'He could come round any minute and start fighting again, so we must act quickly,' Gido said. 'We have to get him to the sea.'

'To the sea?' echoed Leo, almost choking on the smell. 'How?'

'Downriver,' came the abrupt reply.

'What about Rolf?' cried Ginny. 'What shall we do with him?'

'Nothing,' said Maria, and she seemed to be unconcerned. 'He'll be gone by nightfall, if not before.'

'What about the people?' Leo asked, suddenly anxious. 'The owners of the cafe? What happened to them?'

Maria nodded. 'Sleeping,' she said. 'You could say that they are having a little siesta of forgetfulness. Gido can hypnotise in seconds. No harm, sweet dreams. They'll be back at their cooking in no time, just as if nothing had happened here.'

Gido lifted over his shoulder the almost weightless bundle of bones that were now the Stealer, and the others followed as he walked away.

Leo walked alongside Gido. There were questions he wanted to ask. He wasn't sure whether this was the time, but he might not get the opportunity again.

'When Manawl appeared…?' he began.

'You were honoured, the two of you,' Gido replied, before Leo had finished. 'Manawl does not always respond to being called in the way that he did today.'

'But where did he come from?' Leo asked. 'I mean, you always talk about Dreamworld as though it's a place, then he turns up and says he's from Annwn, but that isn't the same as Dreamworld, is it? It's another place, surely.'

'Indeed it is,' Gido said, 'but not in the sense you think of 'place'. It's not about geography, Leo; it's about dimensions. I've told you this before.'

The answer didn't really satisfy Leo. As so often with Gido, Leo felt that his response created even more questions. In fact, there was already another query Leo really wanted to put to him. He wondered if Gido would be angry, if he asked him about it, and decided to ask anyway.

'What did he mean about us working out why you wanted our help so badly?' Gido frowned. 'What do you think he meant?' he asked.

Leo shrugged. 'We were there at the stones, when you were trapped. We heard you. I guess you thought we were the best people for the job of helping.'

'There we are, then,' Gido said, with a finality that stopped Leo questioning further.

Leo knew it wasn't the answer. He knew Manawl had suggested that the Keepers had some motive other than the obvious one. He sighed, knowing he wasn't going to find out yet what it was, and making a promise to himself that he would discover it some time, even if it took an age.

The river was high, due to the rain from the previous day, and even as they reached the path that led through the field and down to the water, more rain was starting, big drops that pattered down and threatened a heavy downpour to come.

Leo looked at Ginny and saw that she was weeping.

'Don't feel sorry for the Stealer,' he said. 'Neptune will look after him. He'll be properly dead, not trapped.'

'Oh, shut up,' she snapped. 'I know all that. I'm not crying for him. I'm crying for the Grolchen, and because we lost the brooch, and because we let the other Stealer get away.'

'Ah, yes,' he said.

There really was plenty to cry about, he thought, and the only thing that was stopping him from joining in was his need to see the end of the Stealer, so that at least he could be sure he wasn't going to suddenly spring back to life, take on another horrible shape, and start struggling again.

Gido waded into the mid-stream, holding the Stealer out in his arms. When the water reached his chest, he stopped wading and began to speak words of magic, calling Neptune's name again and again.

'Why doesn't he just put him in the water and let the river

take him?' Leo asked Maria. 'The river goes to the sea anyway.'

'He can't do that,' Maria answered. 'Neptune must be told that he's coming. We can't leave anything to chance. Between here and the sea, a lot can happen. For all we know, his brother is on the bank, further down, and could pull him out. He's sure to know what we intend doing. If Neptune doesn't know he's on his way, anything could still go wrong for us.'

As if her words had conjured him, they suddenly saw the second Stealer. He stood on a high ledge, further down river, and he held Bos in front of him, dangling him over the water.

'Don't do it!' he screamed, and his voice was almost lost in the sudden rise of the noise of rain. 'Get him out, or the boy goes in.'

Gido threw back his head in a defiant gesture, and continued his incantation. The Stealer on the bank thrust his free arm in the air, whilst Bos hung suspended, eyes bulging with terror. Leo and Ginny gasped when they saw the flash of metal in the Stealer's upraised hand.

'He's using the brooch!' Leo shouted to Gido. 'He's doing something.'

The brooch gleamed, wet and shiny, as a stream of words spilled from the Stealer, in a wild, gabbled attempt to activate its magic. The noise around them grew louder and, sensing it was not only the rain, Ginny looked up.

'Look!' she cried, pointing skywards. 'It's the rooks!'

It made no sense to Leo. He knew that the birds hated rain, but there above them, circling and flapping their wings, was the rook parliament.

'You see!' yelled the Stealer. 'I have called my friends, and they are here to help me.'

He began to wave to the birds, shouting, 'Get them! Get them!'

For a wild, panicky moment, Leo wondered whether the Stealer had actually managed to get the rooks back on his side. He could see that Ginny was wondering the same thing.

'Oh no,' she murmured, covering her head with her arms. 'Not again.'

However, as the rooks flocked together, preparing to fly downward, it became obvious they were not aiming for Gido, or for Maria, or the children. They gathered into the shape of an enormous arrowhead, and, as the rain lashed their wings, they flew down in formation towards the Stealer.

As they plunged downward, they parted into two ranks, and a path opened between them. A huge, beautiful, black and white magpie came right through the middle.

With breathtaking speed and accuracy, it dropped on its target, and, without a pause, lifted the brooch from the Stealer's hand, flew up in a graceful arc, high into the rain-filled sky, and was gone. As one body, the rooks followed.

'Magpies love bright things,' whispered Ginny, amazed at the sight.

The Stealer flung Bos aside and began shaking his fists at the sky, at the disappearing birds.

'You stupid creatures,' he shouted. '*They* are the enemy! Not me! I am your master! Bring it back to me!'

Bos was running from the river as fast as his legs would carry him. The Stealer cast around in fury and despair, and then ran after him. Gido's words were having an effect on the river, and the atmosphere changed. Leo and Ginny glanced at each other. They *felt* Neptune's approach and, with it, the strange excitement of being in the presence of something beyond their understanding. What looked like a high tide was moving up the river to where Gido stood. It moved gently, and stopped just short of him. Then it rose like a huge hand, scooped the Stealer from his arms and retreated down river to the sea.

'Magic,' Leo sighed. 'It's incredible. We did it. We got one of them. But we lost the brooch.'

'You haven't really lost the brooch,' said Maria. She was smiling. 'Don't you know who that was?'

'Who what was?' asked Leo.

'Grolchen,' she said. 'The magpie was Grolchen.'

'What?' Ginny's eyes were round.

'You can't kill a dreamself, only the shape he takes,' she replied. 'I never saw him do a bird before, but that was clever, even for Grolchen. Yes, I must admit, that was clever.'

She turned and called to Gido, who was striding to the bank.

'We'm best be goin'.' She pointed to the sky. 'Moon movin' along.'

Something was happening to her as she spoke, her bun looked wonkier, and her little boots and apron were suddenly reappearing. Gido was striding to the bank, and Ginny saw that he was dry, not soaking wet from his wade in the water. Leo blinked. Gido was changing and, like Maria, he was returning to himself. The multi-coloured waistcoat that almost glowed in the dark flashed at them as he climbed up beside them. He stretched out a hand to shake theirs.

'Good, good,' he said. 'We'll be in touch.'

Maria patted them on the shoulders.

'You'm a good pair. We'll be seein' you agin,' she said.

The next minute, they were gone, and the rain pelted down, and the wind blew a gale, but Leo and Ginny sat on the bus back to Parrog, apart from it, and unconcerned, in their own world, which felt okay.

After all, what was a little rain, after what they'd been through?

'Grolchen'll make sure we find the brooch again, if we're meant to have it,' Leo said to Ginny.

'I expect we'll have to wait for the right time, for the moon and stuff,' she said.

Leo shrugged. 'I'm not sure, Ginny. It can't have left this world. I think it's just a case of keeping our eyes open for it.'

★   ★   ★

'We'll have the big bunch please,' Ginny said. 'She'll like those.'

The lady behind the counter lifted the largest bunch of bright red and orange flowers from the bucket. It had been a difficult decision between them, deciding what to buy Izzy, to say thank-you for having them. Leo argued for giving her a book, or a CD, but Ginny insisted that those were sorts of things Izzy bought for herself all the time.

'But, Leo, she hardly ever treats herself to flowers, and she loves them,' she'd said.

They'd pooled their money beforehand, and now, they left the shop, with Leo carrying their purchase, and he felt good about it.

'If we had bought a book, or a CD, we'd have had to think about which one. This is much easier,' he said, 'and they're really nice.' He laughed. 'You're quite often right about things,' he said. 'Like suggesting that we go to Narberth, and what you said about Gido, at the castle. I was a bit of a prat, really. Shall we walk back along the beach? I want to show you the sea wall before we go. It's incredible.'

They admired the wall for some minutes. Ginny poked around between the stones and slates.

'I was just thinking, this would be a great place to find the brooch,' she said. 'All these little nooks and crannies, remind me of it, and the Grolchen. I don't know why. Don't you have a funny feeling that it's just around the corner?'

'Not especially,' Leo said, 'but I have been thinking about Bos and the Stealer, and what happened. I don't suppose we've seen the last of either of them.'

'I hope we have,' Ginny said. 'Anyway, you'll have to see Bos in school, I expect. As for the other Stealer, ugh! I hope, now that he's on his own, he'll just go somewhere far away.'

'I'm not sure he will,' Leo said. 'I think, if we don't get the brooch back, he might leave us alone, but if we find it again, we might have to use it. That was why Manawl told us the secret.'

A group of gulls flew overhead, coming in from the sea, and their cries made the children look upward.

With a plop, a large bird-dropping spattered on Ginny's shoulder, followed by a second one, which landed right in the middle of the large bunch of flowers. The gulls flew on. The children stared at each other.

'Oh no,' Ginny groaned, looking at the mess on her shoulder. 'This stuff is really hard to get off, and it's in the flowers too!'

Leo looked down into the bunch. Surrounding the colourful blooms was a mass of green leaves.

'It's gone right down to the bottom,' he said. 'There's only a bit on the edges, at the top. Izzy will soon wash it off.'

When they got back, the bouquet of flowers overwhelmed Izzy.

'How thoughtful!' she exclaimed. 'They're beautiful.'

As they gave them to her, they explained hastily what had happened, and she quickly opened the cone of paper they were wrapped in. One by one, she lifted them out, and wiped the messy traces off.

'There's hardly any of the stuff on them,' she said. 'I think you got the worst of it, Ginny. We'll soak your T-shirt. Oh! That's odd!'

The children looked at what she had found. She held it out on her open palm, to show them. It was a small, tin lid. Leo reached out and took it, examining it as though he had never seen such an oddity before, although he knew exactly what it was. He glanced at Ginny. She knew too, he could tell.

'I don't think that came out of a seagull's bottom,' he said.

Izzy laughed. Ginny giggled. Leo smiled, and somewhere, a sound passed from Overworld to Dreamworld, and into the very halls of Annwn, carrying a message of destiny unfolding.